RACHEL RUDE ROWDY

Ginny Kalish

Zephyr Press

TUCSON, ARIZONA

DEDICATION

For Memory 7, the Bow-Legged Trickster, and all the other Kalish Kids who have enriched my life beyond measure.

Rachel Rude Rowdy

Grades 2-6

©2001 by Ginny Kalish

Printed in the United States of America

ISBN 1-56976-127-2

Editor: Bonnie Lewis
Illustrations: Rita Treat
Cover design: Dan Miedaner
Design and production: Sheryl Shetler

Published by Zephyr Press
P.O. Box 66006
Tucson, Arizona 85728-6006
800-232-2187
www.zephyrpress.com
www.i-home-school.com

Library of Congress Cataloging-in-Publication Data

Kalish, Ginny.
    Rachel Rude Rowdy / Ginny Kalish
       p. cm.
    Includes comprehension questions and lesson plans in character development.
    Summary: Jason's plots to get Rachel kicked out of school keep getting turned against him until, in an art therapy class, he learns something about her home life that makes him see her rude behavior in a new light.
    ISBN 1-56976-127-2 (alk. paper)
    [1. Behavior—Fiction. 2. Interpersonal relations—Fiction. 3. Schools—Fiction. 4. Family problems—Fiction.] I. Title.

PZ7.K1252 Rac 2001
[Fic]—dc21   00-065470

ACKNOWLEDGEMENTS

I would like to thank my friends and family who did so much to help me with the book.

I am also very grateful for the good fortune of working with Jenny Flynn at Zephyr Press. Most especially, I thank my husband Marc, whose myriad contributions (not the least of which was making sure that the entire book was not one long dangling participle) ensured that *Rachel Rude Rowdy* finally saw the light of day.

CONTENTS

INTRODUCTION

The best-kept secret to teaching reading is that the more students read, the better readers they become. That discovery was such a joy because it released me from standing in line at the copy machine. I spend my time reading novels, and my students spend their time reading novels. Talk about a win-win situation!

It was when I was reading one particular novel that my dream was born. The back cover explained that the author was a teacher who wrote the book for her students. "I sure wish I could do that," I thought to myself. For several years that was all I did—I thought about it, and then I thought about it some more.

You all know the setting. I was in your basic classroom: four walls and no windows. The acoustical tiles do little to absorb the vibrations. There is a leak in the ceiling from the last rainstorm, and a fight is breaking out in the back corner. Stifled sobs compete with bold laughter as the latest joke makes the rounds. My eyes dart around as I swiftly calculate that there are exactly 29 heads in this room. As a teacher, I had been in this setting for 10 years.

Then, one fall day, my much-hoped-for inspiration made her appearance. I always suspected that she would come, but I had no warning. Suddenly, in a puff of chalk dust during a not-otherwise-inspirational spelling lesson, Rachel Rude Rowdy was created. You see, I had hastily written some words on the blackboard. Billy raised his hand and asked what one of the words was. He said, "It looks like Rachel."

Something inside me clicked, because I told him that was exactly what the word said, "Rachel." I said she must have sneaked into our classroom and written her name on our board. In fact, I further suggested, "Rachel" was probably responsible for many of the mishaps in our classroom. The students were on board from the beginning, and we blamed Rachel indiscriminately for every succeeding mishap. "That Rachel!" we would scoff as we shook our heads.

I was in the shower (watering the idea) when it hit me. I could write a book—a book about Rachel. Then, the best thing happened. I started writing (after I had dried off, of course). The writing of the book was one of the happiest experiences of my life.

Rachel came alive to me. I knew what she was going to do before she did it. When I started typing, it often seemed that my fingers just moved independently. It felt as if Rachel was in control. I did not control her; I merely reported what she was doing. As you will see when you read the book, I was not alone. Many have tried to control our Rachel; none have succeeded. She would wake me up at 4:00 a.m. with her shenanigans.

It actually seemed as if the computer was calling me, "You'd better get in here now. You won't believe what these kids are doing." I must confess that there were times when I was stuck. I had regular Friday meetings with my kids. I'd report where Rachel was last seen and what she was doing. I polled them for ideas about what should happen next. I think this was their favorite part of the week.

I didn't always know what path Rachel would take, but I always knew the message I wanted to impart to my readers. I had a lot of help along the way, but it was Zephyr Press that saw the book as a perfect vehicle for character education.

So, it was back to work to create the lessons you will find at the end of the book. Creating the lessons also gave me a great deal of pleasure. The teacher in me was thrilled to find an opportunity to impart character development within the context of the novel.

My deepest hope is that Rachel comes alive to her readers. By knowing Rachel, you know many people in the world. And by teaching students how to respond to the Rachels of the world—how to respect and even appreciate them, how to empathize with them and show compassion—educators are improving the future of humankind. If this book helps you teach one "Jason" how to take the initiative to see what needs to be done to help someone else, and to do it without anyone telling him to, I will feel happy to have contributed in a small way to that end.

SUGGESTIONS FOR USING THIS BOOK

The Author's Hope

It is my sincere hope that *Rachel Rude Rowdy* facilitates growth in empathy, understanding, and cooperation. I cannot pass up the opportunity to wish you joy as you experience this book with your students. Even though the overall message is serious, as teachers we know there are so many moments when sheer joy takes over and reaffirms why we went into teaching.

Classroom Materials Provided

The novel and accompanying support materials can be used in myriad ways. If you want to extend a lesson or idea, have fun and run with it. Pick and choose what works for you from the classroom-support materials provided for each chapter:

- a set of comprehension questions at the end of each chapter in the novel
- two character-related lessons per chapter (grouped following the novel), complete with discussion questions, summing-up sections, and journal reflections

Tips for Using the Book

There are many ways to use *Rachel Rude Rowdy*. The suggestions below provide one road map, but there is definitely room to experiment.

The Novel

The novel reads well aloud. You may want to share it in that way, chapter by chapter. Students could also read portions of it aloud, with different students assuming the roles of the various characters.

Should you choose to have students read aloud, bear in mind that best practice dictates that students practice before reading in front of the class. Although I would encourage students to participate in oral reading, I suggest that it should be voluntary, to avoid embarrassment.

Questions for Review and Further Thought

The questions at the end of each chapter can be used in oral or written form. Try asking your students to write their own questions, using those provided as a model or springboard.

The Lessons

The two character lessons for each chapter can engage your students actively in the process of character development. Use the discussion and summing-up sections of the lessons to reflect back on the novel or the lessons, and to bridge to the next chapter. Review the summing-up section before starting a new chapter. See page ix for suggestions on involving parents in reflective homework activities.

Journal Reflections

Journaling is the perfect vehicle for self-exploration and reflection. However, you may want to consider using the journal as a dialogue between teacher and student. The journal would also work well as a way to involve parents. Homework assignments could involve sharing student journals at home, where parents and students can make entries in the journal.

Assessment

One method of assessment involves ongoing observation. Jot down baseline observations when you begin presenting the novel. Then, through actual observation, sharing, and journaling, note if students are applying what they have learned about character development.

The lessons for chapter 17 (see pages 112–114) provide two additional assessment activities. The first is an observation game for assessing your students' understanding of the material. The second employs the journals students have been keeping during their study of the novel. Preview the lessons for chapter 17 before introducing *Rachel Rude Rowdy* to decide if and how you will use the journal as a self-assessment activity.

Involving Parents

Involve parents in the *Rachel Rude Rowdy* project and the on-going process of character development by including them in students' homework assignments. Here are some suggestions for involving parents in homework activities. Students—

- retell the story and ask their parents' opinions about the characters' actions
- interview parents to see if, as children, they experienced situations similar to those in the novel
- predict with their parents what they think will happen next in the story or discuss the consequences of choices made by particular characters
- brainstorm solutions with parents
- interview parents for their advice

A Word about Sensitive Issues

In *Rachel Rude Rowdy,* the characters find themselves in difficult and true-to-life situations that may resemble the experiences of some of your students. The novel and activities may bring to light a student's problem or concern. When children share sensitive information, be aware of school policies and refer the child to the school administration, counselor, or nurse to provide appropriate resources to address the problem.

Why Use a Novel to Teach Character Education?

The use of the novel accomplishes many goals. The characters experience moral and ethical dilemmas as part of a naturally evolving story. The lessons arise out of the story, rather than a contrived scenario. A novel also is ripe with opportunities to teach across the curriculum, including literature studies. This format invites children to get to know the characters and identify with aspects of the story that pertain to their own lives.

Finally, this novel can be used to help establish a classroom community of caring individuals—the kind of community that is so important in education.

Why Use Multiple Intelligences?

The lessons are written to tap into students' multiple intelligences. The use of multiple intelligences provides the opportunity to develop our students' intellectual capacities. By utilizing all of the intelligences, we empower students to practice their strengths and improve those intelligences that are not yet as strongly developed. We show students that we value their uniqueness, and we celebrate their diversity.

Where Do I Fit This in My Curriculum?

I would recommend that this book be used to establish a caring community within the classroom. It lends itself to being read aloud and provides activities to extend the reading into character-building activities. Teach material targeted by state standards by implementing discussion or answering questions that parallel the grade-level standards for your class, as inspired by the novel and accompanying lessons. The book can also serve as a vehicle for parental involvement by assigning homework that integrates the novel with child, parent, and teacher interactions.

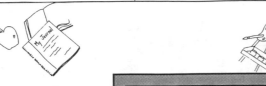

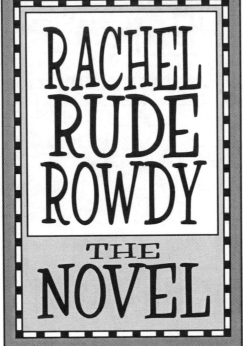

RACHEL
RUDE
ROWDY
THE
NOVEL

CHAPTER 1

READING, 'RITING, AND 'RITHMETIC?

It all started on Friday the 13th. I should have known by the unlucky date what was going to happen. But I didn't. It was my last Friday of freedom. In other words, summer vacation was over and school was going to start the next Monday.

Vacation had been great. I still got up early every morning. Instead of getting ready for school though, I stayed in my pajamas, ate cereal, and watched cartoons until my best friend, Pablo, was ready to play. I can't even remember all of the neat stuff we did that summer. But I do remember that summer as the last time my life was not ruled by the three Rs.

My mom and dad have always said that you go to school to learn the three Rs. They meant reading, 'riting, and 'rithmetic. I could take those three Rs. Actually, I'm pretty good at 'rithmetic. The three Rs that almost ruined my life that year had nothing to do with books. That problem came with curly red hair, freckles, and the name of Rachel Rude Rowdy.

The school was posting the class lists that Friday morning, and Pablo and I were all set to go. We always rode our bikes there to see who our teacher was going to be and which kids were in our class. We were really hoping to be in the same class this year. Ever since we put glue on the girls' seats in first grade, our principal made sure that we were in different classrooms. Luckily, that principal retired after last year, and our hopes were high.

Being together in fifth grade was especially important to us. We knew that we couldn't spend the next summer together, because Pablo's family was going to his grandma's farm. His mother had been planning a family reunion for the past two years. That's why we were so anxious at least to be together as much as possible during the school year.

When we got to school, we couldn't even see the doors. There were so many kids and parents crowding around the lists. Actually, it was sort of fun to see everyone again. And I have to admit that toward the end, vacation did have its boring moments. In a strange way, I was looking forward to school starting.

I was real excited when I finally got to see the class list. I was right. The new principal, Mr. Cheng, didn't know about Pablo and me. We were together! What luck! We even had the teacher who was known for being kind of crazy. Her name was Ms. Williams. Some of the kids who had her last year said that when it was your birthday, she actually stood on your desk and danced as the class sang "Happy Birthday." The way I look at it, if a teacher acts like that, she would never get mad at a kid for acting a little crazy. Fifth grade was going to be the best year of my life. I was sure of it when I saw the class list.

Jason Parker
Pablo Rinaldo
Rachel Rowd

Pablo and I figured we could even live through a year with Rachel in our class. Rachel Rowd was disgusting. More disgusting than any ordinary girl I've ever met. In second grade, she used to spit on our desks when the teacher wasn't looking. That's when we gave her the middle name of Rude. It's hard to remember when we changed her last name from Rowd to Rowdy. I think it was in first grade, when she threw a rock at Mandy Duncan. Poor Mandy had to get 14 stitches in her forehead. Anyway, Rachel Rude Rowdy was the perfect name for the red-headed creature who was going to be in our class.

I wasn't worried, though. I figured that I could put up with anyone, as long as I got to be in class with Pablo. Boy, was I wrong. I was going to learn a lot that year, and Rachel Rude Rowdy, not Ms. Williams, was going to be my teacher.

For Review and Further Thought

☐ Why was Jason excited when he saw the class list?
☐ Describe Rachel. How are you like her? How are you different?

CHAPTER 2

DECISIONS?

Monday morning—the first day of fifth grade. I woke up even earlier than usual. Mom made eggs for breakfast. She usually fusses over my little sister Tisha and me at the beginning of the school year. It lasts about two weeks. Then it's back to cold cereal and making it out of the door without brushing my hair.

This morning I didn't even mind when she kissed me in front of Pablo, who had come over so that we could ride our bikes to school together. I was that excited about being in class with my best friend. At least Mom let me ride my bike. Until this year, she had always insisted on driving me to school on the first day.

We got to school, locked up our bikes, and headed for the playground. It was fun seeing everyone again. On the first day of school, I'm even happy to see the kids I don't like. We shot some baskets, teased the girls on the swings, and were into a great game of keep away when the bell sounded to line up for class.

Pablo and I walked over to our classroom door to get in line to go inside. Everyone was on their best behavior, and most kids were wearing new clothes. Ms. Williams opened the door. "Please come in, children. Welcome to fifth grade. I think fifth graders are old enough to make decisions for themselves, so please find a desk where you would like to sit. I have made name tags for all of you. Once you have decided which desk you want, please take your name tag and put it on your desk so I can learn your names."

All right! I couldn't believe my ears. We were allowed to sit anywhere. That meant we could sit next to anyone we wanted to. Last year, when I was talking too much to my friends, my teacher moved me next to Rachel. It was a good move on the teacher's part because Rachel's the last person I'd want to talk to.

I knew from experience that Rachel always makes this squeaking noise when she works. It isn't loud enough for the teacher to hear—just loud enough to bother the kids around her. She's also messy. She spreads out all of her junk so that half of it ends up on the desk next to hers. That was my desk last year. Then, when she can't find something, she'll accuse her neighbor of taking her things.

It was awful sitting next to her in fourth grade, but now I knew that fifth grade wasn't going to be as bad. "Pablo," I yelled, "over here. Let's sit way in the back, next to each other."

Pablo joined me and we quickly claimed two desks in the back, right next to each other. Ms. Williams took attendance and started explaining the school rules. I've been hearing those same rules every year now since I've been in school, so I took out the baseball cards my dad had given me the night before as a sort of welcome-back-to-school present. Pablo was impressed.

"I wish my dad gave me back-to-school presents," he complained. "Would you trade me a Sammy Sosa and Roger Clemens for my Mark McGwire?" I agreed. I knew it wasn't the perfect trade, but he is my best friend.

Pablo was really smiling now. He was so happy to get that card.

Suddenly, the room seemed very quiet. I looked up and saw that the other kids were all turned around in their seats, staring at us. I had that sinking feeling, you know, like the teacher has been talking to you and you didn't know it. Well, I was right.

"Jason and Pablo, I was just telling the class how exciting it is to learn new things and meet new people. Because you two already seem to know each other so well, I think it would be good for you to have a new experience. Pablo, would you please move over one seat? Rachel, you seem like an interesting person. No one can get to know you, sitting all alone like that. Would you please move and sit between Jason and Pablo?"

All of my hopes for fifth grade started to crumble at that moment. To tell you the truth, I would rather have my mother kiss me in front of the whole class than sit next to Rachel Rude Rowdy again. Sitting next to Rachel was worse than any torture I could imagine. No one should have to put up with her two years in a row.

For Review and Further Thought

☐ Jason made the decision to sit next to Pablo. Did that turn out as he expected? Tell why or why not.

☐ Was the teacher wise to arrange the seating the way she did? Tell why or why not.

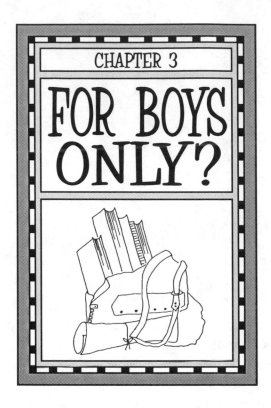

CHAPTER 3

FOR BOYS ONLY?

For the rest of that first day of school, Pablo and I were pretty miserable. Things always seem worse when you have your hopes way up there. We really thought we were going to rule fifth grade, sitting together in the back of the room.

When the dismissal bell finally rang, without saying a word to each other, we both headed towards the boys' bathroom. It's the one place in school where we could get away from teachers—and Rachel Rude Rowdy. Not even Rachel Rude Rowdy would be disgusting enough to go to the boys' bathroom. At least that's what we thought.

We had to wait a few minutes until the rest of the boys cleared out so that we could talk in private. "My life is over," I said. "I can't come to school every day if I have to sit next to HER."

"I know what you mean," Pablo replied. "The whole time Ms. Williams was explaining the class rules, Rachel was burping in my ear."

I was really worried. "If she's burping on the first day of school, when everyone is on their best behavior, can you imagine what she'll do the rest of the week ... the rest of the year? You know, Rachel has always been such a pest. I want this year to be different. It would be pretty funny if this year we were the ones doing the pestering."

"That does sounds like fun, Jason. You always have good ideas. Remember the time Tisha kept sneaking into your room? Your mother didn't believe she would do anything like that. So you put itching powder on your desk, and caught her red-handed. Ha ha. You've got to come up with an idea to really get Rachel. Think!"

"All right, all right. We've got to come up with a plan, a great plan," I agreed.

After a few minutes, I felt the beginning of an idea. "Think about how it feels when everyone in the class knows you've done something wrong," I said.

"If you think it's embarrassing for the whole class to know, imagine if the whole school knows you're in trouble," Pablo shouted.

"Hey, Pablo, that's it! That's just what we need. We have to come up with a plan that's so good that everyone will know about Rachel Rude Rowdy. It'll be the best—knowing we got her before she could get to us!" I was grinning from ear to ear. I always do that when I know I've come up with a brainstorm.

"I can't wait to get started," Pablo said. "What do we do first?"

"We've got to plan this very carefully. I'll go home and write down the things we can do to get Rachel in trouble. In fact, if I think about playing a trick on her, I may begin to be able to say the letter R again without getting depressed."

Pablo seemed really excited. "Jason, I'll call you later tonight, and you can tell me what to do."

"No, we've got to be very careful. You never know when my sister will listen in on the phone. She's been worse than ever lately. I'll think about it tonight. On the way to school tomorrow, I'll tell you the plan."

"Sounds good ..." Pablo stopped. "Oh, no. I forgot that I have a dentist appointment in the morning, so my mom is going to be driving me to school after the appointment."

"That's okay. I'll write down Plan-R and leave it for you." I was really cooking now.

"Where will you leave it?" Pablo asked.

I had to think for a minute. Then I had it. "Right here, in the boys' bathroom. That way we can be sure that Rachel will never find out about it. See this space between the wall and the paper-towel holder? I'll hide the plan in there. You sign out to go to the bathroom right after I do tomorrow morning. Then you can go and read the plan. Pretty soon Rachel Rude Rowdy won't feel like pestering us anymore."

As we went to get our bikes out of the bike rack, Pablo and I were feeling pretty good again. It didn't even bother us when we saw Rachel standing by the flagpole across from the bike rack. Why should she hurry home from school? Her parents were probably happy if she came home late.

For Review and Further Thought

☐ Tell about Plan-R.
☐ Is it a good idea? Tell why or why not.

CHAPTER 4

DOUBLE YOUR PLEASURE?

When I got home, my mom kept following me around asking me about the first day of school. My little sister was worse than usual, and I got sent to my room for telling her to shut up. Actually, it was the first time I was glad to be sent to my room. Now I could begin Plan-R.

I got out a piece of paper. Getting Rachel in trouble shouldn't be too hard. It happens to kids all the time. We just had to be very careful not to let anyone know that Pablo and I were actually planning the things that Rachel would get in trouble for doing. I figured we had to start out with small things, then see what happened.

The first idea was easy. We'd act like we wanted to be friends with Rachel so she wouldn't suspect us. Rachel didn't have any friends, so she couldn't afford to be choosy. Not only doesn't she have any friends, she's the only kid I know who shows up at the school's family picnic by herself.

The plan would be to bring her a pack of gum, and give it to her at the morning recess. A kid like Rachel could not go the whole day without chewing that gum. It's impossible. Chewing gum in our school was a big deal, ever since the PTA had to pay $200 to remove chewed gum from the new chairs in the library. I knew I could count on teachers to kind of freak out when they saw Rachel with gum.

I quickly wrote down the idea for Pablo, and went to hide the paper in my desk. As I was closing my desk drawer, my mom called me to wash up and come down to dinner.

When I got to the table, my sister was busy monopolizing the conversation, as usual. She talked so much I was hardly able to get a word in edgewise—or any other way for that matter. Usually, this really bothered me. Tonight, I didn't even get upset. I felt happy just thinking about Rachel and my outstanding plan.

Tisha was all excited because she had bugged Mom so much that Mom had agreed to be her Girl Scout troop leader this year. "Mommy, doesn't that mean that we get to have the meetings at our house? Can we have a sleepover, too?"

Hearing that, I forced myself to concentrate on the conversation. "Mom, Dad, don't tell me that those goofy little girls are going to be at our house all of the time, doing all of that girl stuff."

"Jason," my mother answered. "They are not goofy. Remember, you're only one year older than your sister. We're going to be doing a lot of interesting things. And, yes, Tisha, we will be able to have a Girl Scout sleepover."

"I won't be able to stand it," I protested.

"Enough of that," my father said to me. Then he turned to my mother and said, "Dear, perhaps we could arrange for Jason to spend the night at Pablo's when the Girl Scouts sleep over."

It was a relief to know that at least my dad could understand a boy's point of view. As far as I was concerned, the only kind of Girl Scout I wanted in my house was the kind that came on a box of cookies.

As we were finishing dinner, Tisha rattled on and on about her Girl Scout troop the whole time. She was listing the names of the girls in her troop. When I heard one of the names I started to gag on my hamburger.

"Who did you just say? What was the name of that kid you just said?"

Mom answered, "Rachel Rowd. I know she's in fifth grade, but she's only nine. Her parents must have had her start school a year early. She must be very smart."

"Her parents are the smart ones. If I were her parents, I'd make her go to school early, too," I commented. "Anything to get her out of the house. She's not really going to be coming over here, is she Mom?"

"Yes, Jason, she is. And, you will be polite. I've seen how the children at school treat her. All she needs is a little kindness," my mother explained.

"Ha! You wouldn't say that if you had to sit next to her..."

"Enough!" Dad interrupted. "Help your mother clear the table, and then go do your homework."

I could tell by the tone of his voice that it would be pointless to argue. My dad has a way of looking at you ... you know when he means business. I cleared the table, did the rest of my homework and got ready for bed. When I fell asleep, I had sweet dreams ... dreams of sweet, sticky gobs of gum.

The next day, I was anxious to get to school and start my plan. I was locking up my bike just as Mrs. Rinaldo dropped off Pablo.

"Jason, did you think up a plan?" Pablo shouted.

"Sshhh, you'll blow the whole thing if anyone hears us," I warned him. "Besides, I think it'll be more fun to keep leaving notes. You know, like they do on TV. Just be sure to check the spot I told you about. I'll leave something there for you every day, and you can do the same if you have any questions."

"I can't wait to go to the bathroom. Ha ha!" Pablo chuckled.

"Yeah, I know what you mean. In fact, I think I'll go in there right now..." I said, and headed straight for the bathrooms.

When I walked in, I was lucky. No one was in there yet, so it was easy to place the folded-up plan behind the paper towel holder, just where I told Pablo it would be. Then I flushed a toilet and pretended to wash my hands, so if anyone came in they wouldn't suspect anything.

The bell rang and we lined up to go to our classrooms. Ms. Williams took attendance and lunch count. We said the Pledge, then we had a math paper to do. I could hear Rachel making little burping noises the whole time. She must have finished her paper early, because she got up and signed out to the bathroom. When she came back in, she bumped into my desk and knocked my paper on the floor. When Ms. Williams looked over, Rachel said, "Oh, how clumsy. I'm so sorry, Jay."

Everyone in the fifth grade knew that if there was one thing that I hated, it was being called Jay. Rachel always called me Jay. I decided not to let it get to me, knowing that later that day Rachel would not be feeling so cheerful.

We checked our math papers and were assigned to read the next lesson in our books. It was then that Pablo made his move. He signed out for the bathroom, and I winked at him as he left. I could feel the pack of gum I had put in my pocket before I left for school. It wouldn't be much longer now.

We felt pretty happy as we walked in line to the lunchroom. As usual, lunch was gross. They called what they put between the buns a hamburger, but it sure didn't taste like one. Anyway, most kids just ate the dessert, dumped their "hamburgers," and went out to recess. That's exactly what Pablo and I did.

That's when we put Plan-R into action. Pablo and I went up to Rachel. She had found some dead worms and was pretending to make spaghetti for some first graders. Even the first graders thought she was weird! Anyway, I began, "Rachel, I know I haven't been exactly friendly in the past. But, now that we're in fifth grade, I think we should act more grown-up. Just to show you there are no hard feelings, I'd like to share my gum with you."

"Yeah, me too," Pablo echoed.

"Thank you, Jay. Thank you, Pablo," Rachel said, taking gum from both of us. "Would you care for some of my spaghetti?"

Pablo and I stared at each other for a minute, shook our heads no, and walked away, trying not to laugh out loud.

We could hardly wait to get back in class and see Rachel get in trouble for chewing gum. We waited all through our spelling lesson—no gum. Then we had social studies—no gum. The next class was P.E., so we sort of forgot about Rachel and concentrated on the volleyball game we were playing.

When we came in from P.E., it was silent-reading time. "Jason and Pablo, I'd like to speak to both of you out in the hall, now!" Ms. Williams said, as everyone was getting settled with a book. The three of us went out into the hall.

Ms. Williams seemed pretty upset. I'd be upset too, if I had a kid like Rachel in my class. Unfortunately, Rachel wasn't the reason our teacher was angry. "Boys, I'm very disappointed in you. It's only the second day of school, and already you've broken a very important school rule."

Pablo and I just stood there with our mouths open. What was she talking about? Then she explained.

"When you were at P.E. I was trying to adjust Rachel's desk for her, like she had asked me to do. While I was doing it, I noticed chewing gum stuck to the bottom of each of your desks. I also found empty gum wrappers in your desks. One of the other students told me that they saw you both together with a pack of gum at recess. You know it's against school rules to chew gum. For the rest of this week, instead of going to recess, you two will come in and scrape gum from the tables in the cafeteria. Maybe then you'll learn the importance of respecting school property and following school rules."

We were so surprised we couldn't even say anything. We just shook our heads and went back to our seats. When we sat down Rachel whispered to us, "What's the matter, Jay? Pablo? Looks like you've gotten yourselves into a sticky situation."

We knew right then that getting Rachel was going to be a little harder than we had first thought.

For Review and Further Thought

☐ Why do you think Plan-R turned out the way it did?
☐ Have you ever planned something that turned out very differently from what you had expected? Tell about it.

CHAPTER 5

IF THERE ARE FIREWORKS, CAN INDEPENDENCE DAY BE FAR AWAY?

When I got home from school my mother said she wanted to have a "little talk." I always know something I'm not going to like is going to happen when she says that.

"Jason, now that you're in fifth grade, you need to start developing good study habits. Your father and I have decided that the best way to do this is to have a homework time set aside every day. When you come home from school, you can have a snack, and then we want you to go to your room and do your schoolwork right away."

"But, Mom," I pleaded, "what about playing with my friends?"

"You can do that after your homework," she said.

Sometimes my parents get what they think is a wonderful new idea, and there is no way to change their minds. But, if I don't put up a fuss, they let up after a few weeks. I decided this was one of the times not to argue, so I ate some "healthy" oatmeal cookies instead. Mom was still trying to be Supermom. The first week of school is rough on all of us. Then I took my backpack and went to my room to do my homework.

I closed my door to make sure that my nosy sister wasn't spying on me. Then I emptied my backpack and started searching for the school handbook. I just had to find a rule for Rachel to break that would get her in *big* trouble. Even scraping gum for a week would be worth it if we could get Rachel. I still couldn't figure out how our plan had backfired. It seemed so perfect when I thought of it. Well, no use crying over spilled milk, as my grandmother would say. On to bigger and better things.

Finding the handbook, I read all of the things kids were not allowed to do at school. It would have saved them a lot of time to just print the things kids *were* allowed to do.

This was not going to be so easy. How could I get Rachel to fight? How could I get her to bring a weapon to school? How could I get her to use unacceptable language? How could ... Wait a minute.

An idea started to form in my mind. I might not be able to get her to actually bring a "weapon" to school, but I still had a firecracker I had found on the playground. If Ms. Williams found that in Rachel's desk, it would surely lead to some pretty interesting fireworks!

I was humming to myself as I wrote out the plan for Pablo. This hour of doing homework in my room just might be a good idea after all.

I folded my copy of the new plan and put it in my backpack. It would be safe there for a few hours. My sister had been worse than usual about snooping through my things, so I had to be real careful not to let her discover the firecracker. I had it hidden in with the supplies for my model airplanes. I knew Tisha would never look there; Mom wouldn't either.

I waited until bedtime before transferring the firecracker to my backpack. I wanted to be sure no one would come in my room. My patience paid off. At bedtime, Tisha was screaming because she couldn't find her Girl Scout pin, and she had Mom and Dad looking all over for it. I knew it was safe to go to my closet. Using my flashlight, I located the shoe box where I keep my model junk. I got

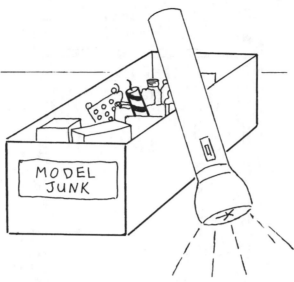

nervous, because I didn't see the firecracker right away. But, when I moved things around, I saw it lying there, waiting to help me start my own Independence Day. Independence from being pestered by Rachel Rude Rowdy.

Suddenly, I realized that for our plan to work without making our teacher suspicious, we needed to wait a few days before taking any action. At the beginning of the school year, kids are usually on their best behavior. Ms. Williams might get suspicious if a lot of behavior problems started happening all at once. Waiting wouldn't be too bad. Just knowing Rachel would really get it almost made the waiting fun. I took the firecracker and my plan out of my backpack. I returned the firecracker to the shoe box in my closet. I hid the plan in the secret compartment of my desk. I decided it was a good idea to keep my original plan there—it would make me happy just to reread it often. I could write out a copy for Pablo in the morning.

For Review and Further Thought

- [ ] What did Jason choose to do instead of homework, up in his room? What might happen because of this choice?
- [ ] What do you think will happen in the next chapter? Give reasons for your answer.

CHAPTER 6

THE COUNTDOWN?

Before breakfast the next day I wrote Pablo a quick note to let him in on my great idea. I felt just like an undercover agent as I explained about the firecracker and where it was hidden. I told him that if we were lucky, Rachel might even get in so much trouble she'd get taken out of our class and we wouldn't have to sit next to her anymore. That would really be the icing on our "Pester Rachel" cake. I ended the note by explaining that we would wait a few days before using my idea.

Mom didn't seem to notice that I was late getting down to breakfast—Tisha was still having a fit about her dumb Girl Scout pin. Mom was so concerned about that precious pin, I even got to eat cold cereal for breakfast. The day was off to a great start.

When I got to school, I quickly went to the boys' bathroom and left the note for Pablo behind the paper-towel holder. Then I went to see if any of the guys had started the usual before-school dodgeball game. The game had started all right, but what I saw sure didn't make me want to play. As I glanced at the court, I glimpsed a flash of curly red hair. That could mean only one thing. Rachel Rude Rowdy was playing. That girl could ruin a person's whole life! The new principal had decided that students could play in any game they wanted while they were on school property. Not so bad? Dodgeball is dodgeball, right? Wrong! Not when Rachel Rude Rowdy plays. You see, RRR picks her nose all the time. She sticks her "findings" on her shoes. Nobody ever tries to get RRR out, because they don't want to pick up a ball that has touched her shoes. I decided to skip the dodgeball game. Instead, I just kind of wandered around until the bell rang to let us know that it was time to line up for school.

When we got into our classroom, the principal announced over the loudspeaker that later in the day we were going to have an important assembly. I love assemblies. It doesn't really matter what they're about, anything that lets you miss schoolwork is worthwhile to me. At least that's the way it works with most assemblies.

Maybe my brain was still on summer vacation or something, because I still hadn't realized that with Rachel Rude Rowdy in your class, even assemblies can turn out wrong. Don't get me wrong, the assembly was great. There was a guy from NASA—you know, the space center. He talked all about the astronauts and their experiences, and space camp for kids. We even got to touch a real spacesuit and he gave out samples of space ice cream.

The guy from NASA wasn't the problem. Rachel was. During a real neat slide show about weightlessness, our teacher wasn't paying much attention to us. She was busy talking to Mr. LaMar, the sixth-grade teacher. Have you ever noticed how teachers expect kids to be quiet during assemblies and then they talk more than the loud kids? Anyway, while Ms. Williams was busy yakking, I heard these really strange noises coming from the row in front of me. You guessed it: Rachel. She was putting her left hand under her right armpit and pumping her elbow up and down. I have to admit, she was doing a great job of making armpit noises, and I was kind of smiling to myself. I stopped smiling when we got back to our room. Ms. Williams said that we had embarrassed her by making rude noises in the assembly, and gave us two extra pages of math homework.

Even though I knew that Rachel was to blame, I don't believe in telling on other kids. Just last week, I saw Heather take Lilia's new ballpoint pen. It was the kind that had those sparkly things floating in water inside of the top. Ms. Williams asked the class if anyone knew about the disappearance of Lilia's pen. I didn't tell, even when Ms. Williams made all of us empty our pockets. It wasn't because I like Heather, I just don't believe in tattling. My sister tattles on me constantly, so I've made up my mind I'm not going to be like that. Anyway, the whole class ended up with two extra pages of math homework because of Rachel.

I was not very happy when I got home. Scraping old gum from lunch tables is not exactly my idea of a good time. I became even more unhappy when I saw what was going on in my house. It seems the reason everyone was searching for the Girl Scout pin was that today was Girl Scout troop day and the meeting was at our house. It almost made me happy about the "go to your room and do your homework right after school" rule. At least my mother let me take some cookies and milk to my room today. Usually no food is allowed upstairs.

I dragged myself upstairs trying to balance the glass of milk and my backpack. As I went down the hallway to my room, I almost dropped everything when I saw who was there. Standing right outside of my bedroom was Rachel Rude Rowdy.

"Hi, Jay. Wasn't that a great assembly we had at school today?" Rachel asked me.

"Yeah," I replied, "especially when we all got extra homework because of you! What are *you* doing in *my* house and standing by *my* room?" I yelled at her.

She looked at me like she thought I was dumb or something. "You do know what a Girl Scout uniform is. I happen to be a member of your sister's Girl Scout troop. I came upstairs looking for the bathroom and I guess I got a little confused."

"Confused?" I shrieked. "How can you be confused between a bedroom and a bathroom?"

Rachel took a few steps toward me so that she was so close to me our faces were almost touching. She opened her mouth to say something, and she shot a dot of spit onto my cheek. Rachel always does that when she talks and it's not an accident. Before she could even speak I made a fist and was about to give Rachel what she deserved when my mother appeared. "Rachel, we need you back downstairs now. You and Jason can visit another time."

I ran into my room, checked my desk, and breathed a big sigh of relief. My plans were still in the secret compartment, just where I had left them.

Rachel was making it awfully tough to wait. I really wanted to get even with her for being such a pest. But I wanted to make sure not to make any mistakes. Whenever I want to feel good, I draw. Sometimes I don't know what to say, but I always know what to draw. I love drawing, and my mom says I'm pretty good at it, too. I calmed myself down by drawing a picture of Rachel with a firecracker in her hand, with the fuse blazing brightly.

For Review and Further Thought

- ☐ Even though the assembly at school was great, Jason didn't have a good day. Why not?
- ☐ What makes Jason feel calm? What do you do to calm yourself down?

CHAPTER 7

BACKFIRE?

Even though I was anxious to "explode" my plan, it wasn't too hard to concentrate on school that week. We were getting ready for Field Day. Field Day is one of the best days of the whole year. We spend the whole day outdoors competing in different athletic events. The week before Field Day is used to practice the events. My favorite is the relay race. Pablo and I got to be on the same team this year, and I knew we could win. Two other kids from our class, Simon and Liu, made up the rest of our team. We were fast, and I knew the only real competition we had was from Mrs. Garcia's fifth-grade class. The kids in her room had beaten my team last year, and I really wanted to win this time.

Practice races were scheduled every afternoon that week. On Monday, we were in the lead, but Simon dropped the baton just as he was about to pass it to me. Oh, I know it seems simple enough to pass a baton. I mean, it's just a hollow tube, and it's not heavy. The problem is that when you pass it, you're running and sweating and sometimes it slips. Anyway, Simon's dropping the baton allowed Mrs. Garcia's team to win. I really didn't mind very much. Sometimes when you think it's going to be easy to win, you get too confident and don't try hard enough. I was hoping that would happen to the other kids. Tuesday's practice made me think I was right. We really killed them. Wednesday was the same. Thursday was not so great. Just as Simon was pulling out in the lead, Rachel decided to play cheerleader. She did a cartwheel right on the corner of the track and tripped Simon as he passed by. It was a clear case of tripping to anyone who was watching carefully. However, when we tried to protest, Mrs. Garcia's class said we were being poor sports. The teachers declared Mrs. Garcia's team the winner. I was furious. Rachel was turning out to be much more of a pain in the neck than I had imagined. Little did I know that she was just warming up. This was not just a practice for the relay team, it was a practice in troublemaking for Rachel.

The race that really counted for us was the next Monday. Unfortunately, the race that really counted for Rachel was this Friday.

As you can imagine, we were pretty excited by Friday afternoon. We had won twice, and Mrs. Garcia's class had won twice. I figured that if we beat them on Friday, maybe they would lose their confidence for next week's race. Simon, Liu, Pablo, and I got in a circle and put our hands on top of each other's. We had made up a little team yell—we all shouted, "Go Williams!" as we raised our hands up in the air.

We lined up at the starting line. Simon was first. The whistle blew and he was off. He was a little slow and passed off the baton after the other team did. I wasn't worried though. Simon was our slowest runner. I knew catching up wouldn't be a problem. Liu was next. She closed up the difference and was running neck and neck with the other team. They both passed off the batons at the same time. This was great. Pablo was fast, and he ran next. Just as I thought he would, he pulled out in the lead. All I would have to do was keep the lead and our team would win. He passed me the baton smoothly, and I was running my best. My arms were pumping up and down,

up and down. Our team won the relay! All the kids from Ms. Williams' class were jumping up and down and yelling. We were really happy, especially me. At least I was happy for one brief moment, until disaster hit.

Sound confusing? Believe me, you aren't the only one confused. You see, whenever I won a race, I would do what I called the "Jason Jig." I would take the baton and hit my heel really hard with it. Everyone knew that was my winning trademark. Just like always, as soon as I crossed the finish line, I did the "Jason Jig." Only this time, something strange happened. As the baton hit my heel, I noticed, out of the corner of my eye, something slip out of the hollow baton and onto the ground. While the other kids were still celebrating, I bent down to see what it was.

A firecracker! Not just any firecracker, but my firecracker. I couldn't believe my eyes. I was so shocked I couldn't even think straight. I looked around, to make sure that no one was watching me. I knew only too well that a kid could get into *big* trouble for having a firecracker at school. I quickly bent down, picked it up, and stuffed it in the pocket of my shorts. Then, I glanced around to make sure I hadn't been discovered, and I got into line with the rest of the class. I let loose a huge sigh of relief when we got back to the classroom.

After the students were seated and quiet, Ms. Williams had an important announcement. She told the class that Rachel had reported that her new cat's-eye marble was missing. None of the kids claimed to know anything about it. Ms. Williams then said the words that made my heart sink, "Everyone, empty your pockets, please." As I slowly reached down to turn my pockets inside out, I just didn't know what to do. How could I explain that the firecracker was mine, but I shouldn't be the one to get into trouble for bringing it to school? I decided to say nothing. Ms. Williams, however, had no trouble deciding what she was going to do. She took me immediately to the principal's office.

Having fireworks on school property is a real big deal. I knew that when I had decided that Rachel should be caught with one in her possession. As I sat waiting to talk to Mr. Cheng, I felt sick. It felt like the little rockets you see on the Fourth of July were going off in my stomach. It wasn't supposed to be like this. Rachel was supposed to be the one here, and I was supposed to be the one celebrating.

When I finally went into the principal's office, things went from bad to worse. After explaining to me the importance of following school rules, Mr. Cheng asked me if I had anything to say for myself.

Now, this was pretty tricky. Naturally, I wanted to explain that I had nothing to do with the firecracker being at school. While I was waiting to talk with the principal, I had a lot of time to think. I was trying to figure out what had happened. During the Girl Scout meeting at my house, while Rachel was "looking for the bathroom," she must have sneaked into my room and somehow found my firecracker. At first, I wanted to explain all of this to the principal. Just as I opened my mouth to start, I began to wonder. Maybe my punishment would be worse if I told what I had been planning. It might be better to let Mr. Cheng think I was just a mischievous fifth-grade boy bringing a firecracker to school. I sadly decided to offer no excuse for my behavior and to try to take my punishment bravely.

That was not an easy job. After a 30-minute lecture, the principal announced that I was disqualified from Field Day next week. While all of the other kids were outside having a great time, I was to sit at a desk in a corner of the office and do schoolwork. This was called an in-house suspension. It seemed that I had not only miscalculated the punishment for having a firecracker, I had also been very wrong when I was dreaming about who would receive that punishment. Just as I was fighting hard not to cry, Rachel walked past the principal's office and waved in at me. She had a big smile on her face. I couldn't believe how much trouble I was in ... and I hadn't even done anything yet.

I was mad! My feelings were like a fire that starts slowly, then catches and explodes. In my mind, I aimed that explosion at Rachel. I had started out just trying to have fun. But now it was more. Rachel was causing my problems. I was going to solve them by getting Rachel Rude Rowdy kicked out of school.

For Review and Further Thought

☐ After the relay race, what fell out of Jason's baton? What did he do with it? What do you think he should have done?

☐ When Ms. Williams (the teacher) discovered what fell out of Jason's baton, what happened? Did Jason deserve this punishment? Tell why or why not.

CHAPTER 8

DOES LAUNDRY LIE?

Mr. Cheng had given me a behavior report form to have signed by my parents. I thought they were pretty upset when Tisha squealed about the problem I had at school with the gum stuck on the desks. I couldn't imagine how upset they'd be when they saw that behavior report. I just couldn't face them about the firecracker. I carefully folded the report into a very small square and put it in my jeans' pocket. I was feeling pretty sad as I went to get my bike. As I unlocked by bike, I realized that I was late and my mother was probably wondering where I was. I rode home as quickly as I could.

"Jason, where on earth have you been? I was really starting to get worried about you," my mother said as I came through the front door.

I hardly knew what to say. I wasn't ready to discuss the firecracker problem, but I did have enough sense to realize that lying would only get me in more trouble.

"Today was the last day of practice before Field Day next week," I said. "I guess I just lost track of time."

"Have you forgotten what today is?" Mom continued. "The Girl Scouts are having a sleepover at our house tonight."

I guess having one horrible thing happen to you can make you forget about another horrible thing that's about to happen.

"Aw, Mom, I can't stand being in the same house with all those giggling girls."

"I know, Jason," Mom said, "that's why I called Pablo's mom and asked her if you could spend the night at their house. She's having company for dinner, but she said it would be fine for you to come over after you eat. I'd like you to take a shower now and get all packed so you can go right over after dinner. When you come downstairs, please be sure to bring me the laundry hamper. I'm going to try to finish a load of wash before all of the Girl Scouts get here."

Gee, my luck is changing, I thought to myself. I don't have to hang around here with all the Girl Scouts tonight. I went up to my room and packed my things for Pablo's house. Then I went into the bathroom to take a shower. I put my dirty clothes in the laundry. I even remembered to set the laundry basket outside the door to take down to my mother when I was done. By now, I was feeling pretty cheerful and I started singing in the shower. I love the way my voice echoes when I sing in the shower. I even decided to wash my hair. Mom hadn't told me to, but I figured it wouldn't hurt to put a little effort into staying on her good side. After all, it was pretty nice of her to call Pablo's mom to let me spend the night.

Usually I'm in and out of the shower pretty quick. Today was different. I was feeling happy about spending the night at Pablo's, and I was just taking my time. On the other hand, Mom was in a hurry to get everything ready for Tisha's Girl Scout sleepover. Instead of waiting for me to bring the laundry to her, she decided to come upstairs herself. She must have been happy when she saw the laundry basket outside the door, all ready to go.

Mom has a little routine she does when she's getting ready to do the wash. First she dumps all of the clothes on the floor. Then she checks for stains and for stuff left in the pockets. Once I had left a marker in my pocket and it ruined two new shirts. That's why Mom always checks the pockets. Another time, Mom had found one of my homework assignments in my pocket. She had thrown it away without realizing what it was. I made her promise not to throw away any papers without reading them first. She must have been thinking about that promise as she unfolded and read the behavior report I had hidden in my pocket.

Just thinking about it gives me the creeps. First, I got a behavior report because my firecracker plan backfired. Then, Mom found the behavior report because I made her promise to read stuff she finds in my pocket instead of just throwing it away. If things kept going like this, I'd be in big trouble.

My dad had promised to come home early from work that day so that he could help with the sleepover. I was just drying off when I heard Dad walk in the door. Through the vent in the bathroom you can clearly hear conversations in the front hall.

"Just look at what I found in Jason's pocket. I asked him why he was late coming home from school and he didn't say anything about this!" I could hear my mom saying to my dad, "I'm starting to get very concerned about him."

"Sometimes children like to test the rules," Dad answered. "When I was his age, I got into trouble for taking cookies out of other kids' lunches. My parents taught me a lesson, and that's what we have to do with Jason."

As I got dressed, I decided my best bet would be to try to make it out of the house before they had time to start asking questions. I tried to smile as I went downstairs.

"Bye, Mom. Bye, Dad. I'm not hungry, so I'm just going to head over to Pablo's ..."

"Not so fast, young man," my father said. "We need to have a little talk. Your mother tells me you were late getting home today."

"Uh, yeah, I guess I was."

Now this was getting pretty complicated. I really didn't know what would be worse. Should I just tell them everything at once, or give it to them a little piece at a time? From the looks on their faces, they weren't ready for the whole thing at once. I made the decision to start out slowly.

"I was practicing for relay races with my team and sort of lost track of the time. Can I go to Pablo's now?"

Wrong! I had been wrong all day. I don't know why I thought this conversation would be any different.

"Jason Parker! How can you stand there and pretend nothing has happened?" My mom was yelling now. The yelling part was just the beginning.

My dad went on to explain, "Jason we're disappointed in the way you have been behaving lately. You have gotten into trouble twice already at school, and the year has just started. The biggest part of the problem is that you didn't tell us the truth right away."

They continued to talk to me about how important it is to tell the truth.

It was pretty painful waiting for the discussion to end and wondering what my punishment was going to be. It was even worse than I expected. I was grounded for one month—starting tonight. Don't get me wrong, I knew the punishment was going to be serious, but to have it start that very night, the night of the Girl Scout sleepover, was almost too much to stand.

I ate a quick dinner at the kitchen table. They didn't even allow me to call Pablo and explain what happened. My mother called Pablo's house while I was eating and simply told them that there had been a change of plans. I went up to my room, lay on my bed, and stared at the ceiling. I could hear the doorbell ringing and the sound of my sister's voice as she screeched hello to her friends. I have to admit I was feeling pretty sorry for myself, and just when I was about to cry, I heard a knock at my door.

"Who is it?" I demanded.

The door flew open. There stood Rachel Rude Rowdy with a big grin on her face.

"Hi, Jay Jay. What happened today after the relay race?"

"None of your business," I mumbled as I threw an old slipper at her. But Rachel moved too quickly. She left and closed the door before the slipper found its target.

The rest of the night was miserable. The girls had their sleeping bags spread out all over the family room, making it impossible to watch TV. I decided not to risk going downstairs for a snack. I was so disgusted with Rachel, I didn't want to take a chance on seeing her again. I just stayed in my room and thought about my problems.

Before I finally went to sleep, I was sure of two things. First, I was sure that I didn't want to get into any more trouble at school and at home. I really didn't like feeling that I'd disappointed my parents. Second, I was sure that I had to get even with Rachel Rude Rowdy!

For Review and Further Thought ⁇

- ☐ The night of the Girl Scout sleepover, Jason stayed in his room and thought about his problems. What are his problems? Who's causing his problems?
- ☐ Choose one of Jason's problems and tell how you would try to solve it.

CHAPTER 9

DO I SMELL A GOOSE COOKING?

The whole next week was pretty rotten. All of the other kids got to go outside and have fun participating in Field Day activities. Not only did I miss Field Day on Monday, but all week long I had to sit at a small desk in the school office and do schoolwork. As if that weren't bad enough, I still couldn't play with my friends after school because I was grounded. Ms. Williams kept bringing me packets of work, but I still felt bored. Studying books and being around live people are two very opposite things. Sitting at that small desk, which must have been borrowed from the first grade, I had a different view of things. I began to see things I hadn't noticed before.

For instance, I knew that if someone in the office wanted to speak to our teacher, first we heard a "beep" in the classroom, then we heard the announcement. If the teacher needed to call the office, she pushed a little button and waited for someone in the office to answer. What I never knew was that when the teacher pushed that little button, a buzzer went off in the office.

The first time I heard the buzzer I jumped, because it surprised me. The school secretary went to her desk and pushed a button, then asked if she could help the teacher who had called. There was no reply. The secretary went back to work. The buzzer went off a few seconds later. The secretary asked if she could help. Again, no reply. This happened three more times. The secretary went into Mr. Cheng's office to tell him what was happening. Just as she was explaining that the speaker system had a problem, I saw Rachel dash out of the building, headed for the playground. Mr. Cheng came out of his office and looked all around. He told his secretary that all of the children were outside for Field Day, so the problem had to be mechanical. He told her to call a repairman. As she was looking for the repairman's phone number, I wanted to tell her it would work only if the repairman knew how to fix Rachel Rude Rowdy. Somehow, I didn't think she'd believe me.

The next day there was a substitute for the music teacher. Pablo told me that Rachel had managed to get her hands on the seating chart. Our music teacher had all of our names written on plastic notes. She arranged our "notes," or name tags, on the seating chart. Rachel had rearranged our chart for that day. Pablo said the substitute got mad at the kids because she thought they were switching seats. I asked Pablo how he knew that Rachel had done it. Besides knowing that she would do something like that, Pablo said he figured it out when Rachel was the only one sitting where her note said she should be. The silly substitute even made Rachel her official helper because she was being so cooperative.

Now, I do have to admit, even I was impressed by Rachel's creativity. Oh, I was still determined to see her kicked out of school. I just couldn't bring myself to have Pablo rat on her. As I've said before, I don't believe in telling on other kids, even if the kid is Rachel. As it turned out, I didn't have to worry about telling on her. In the end, Mr. Cheng always found out who caused the trouble. I could just sit back and enjoy watching Rachel "cook her own goose," as Dad would say.

I didn't have to wait long before Rachel was in really big trouble. As a matter of fact, something happened on the very first day I was allowed back into the classroom.

It seems Rachel had wanted to be first in line to go to lunch. It's kind of hard to be first in line, even for Rachel, when you have a kid like Heather in your class. Heather sits by the door and she's always first in line. She also pushes and pinches if you try to get in front of her. Anyway, Rachel finally beat Heather into the lunch line. Sure enough, Heather tried to push her back. It was kind of fun to watch. It got even better when Rachel got so mad she grabbed the fire extinguisher from the wall. She let Heather have it, spraying her from head to toe.

Rachel was sent to the principal's office. Mr. Cheng was so angry that we could hear him yelling at Rachel as we walked to lunch. "If you break one more rule, young lady, you will be suspended from this school."

When I got to the lunchroom, I realized that I was smiling for the first time all week.

For Review and Further Thought

- ☐ How did Jason feel at the end of the week? Tell why. Have you ever felt the same way?
- ☐ What finally makes Jason smile? Do you like Jason in that moment? Tell why or why not.

CHAPTER 10

NEGATIVE ATTENTION?

My school year wasn't exactly getting off to a great start. I don't think Ms. Williams was having her best year either. Having students who are always in trouble causes problems for the teacher, too, I suppose. Ms. Williams had told us that she had taken a college course during the past summer—she was studying to become a counselor. At first, I thought it would be pretty weird to have your own teacher as a camp counselor, but I soon learned that wasn't the kind of counseling Ms. Williams was studying.

After the fire extinguisher incident, Ms. Williams had the counseling textbooks out on her desk. She would often read them during our silent-reading time. Heather, who was always looking for a way to impress the teacher, asked Ms. Williams to explain to us some of the things she was studying. Ms. Williams told the class that she was reading a chapter about poor self-esteem and the types of behaviors kids have in order to receive what is called negative attention.

She told us that everyone needs attention in order to live. People need attention just like they need food and water. Some people just don't know how to get attention for themselves in the right way. They misbehave in order to get negative attention. This usually happens when people don't feel very good about themselves. When a person doesn't feel very good about himself or herself, well, that's called poor self-esteem.

Ms. Williams must have decided that Rachel Rude Rowdy was suffering from poor self-esteem, because after school the next day Rachel's mom showed up for a conference. She was waiting outside of the classroom just as we were being dismissed.

Pablo was getting a drink in the hall when he signaled me.

"What's going on?" I asked him.

"Shh! Be quiet and listen," Pablo told me. "This is the perfect spot to hear what's going on inside. I have to go now, but you've got to check this out, Jason."

Pablo was right. I could hear Mrs. Rowd talking. I hung around, pretending to be very thirsty, but I was spying on their conference.

Mrs. Rowd explained that Mr. Rowd couldn't come to the meeting. Mrs. Rowd seemed very nervous and upset. She kept twisting a tissue in her hand, and she never really looked at Ms. Williams when she was speaking.

Ms. Williams explained that Rachel had been displaying such negative behavior that she was close to being suspended from school. When Mrs. Rowd heard that, she started to cry.

"Now we're not here to make you upset," I heard Ms. Williams explain, "we're here to try to help Rachel."

"I'd really like to help Rachel. I love her very much. But her father doesn't make a lot of money, and he doesn't give me any extra," Mrs. Rowd explained. "I don't have a job; I don't seem to be very good at anything. I just couldn't afford to send her for extra help."

"I know getting help can be expensive," Ms. Williams said. "However, some people who help only charge what you can afford to pay ..."

Just when the conversation was getting interesting, Mr. Cheng came walking down the hall. I ran out of the building as quickly as I could. I waited outside to see if I could hear any more. I could hear voices, but I really couldn't make out what they were saying.

Rachel was playing with some rocks in a corner of the parking lot while she was waiting for her mother. She didn't notice me, so I waited around to see if anything interesting happened.

After about five minutes, Mrs. Rowd came out of the building and headed for her car. I could hear her as she scolded Rachel, "Get in the car, Rachel. We mustn't be late getting home. I have to start cooking your father's dinner. You know how upset he gets when dinner isn't ready on time. And, we don't need to tell him about these little problems at school. It would only upset him. You know what happens when he gets upset."

Little problems at school? If these were little problems, it made me wonder what Rachel's family thought a big problem was.

For Review and Further Thought

☐ What clues in this chapter help us learn about Rachel's family? What do we learn?

☐ Does this information change the way you feel about Rachel? Tell why or why not.

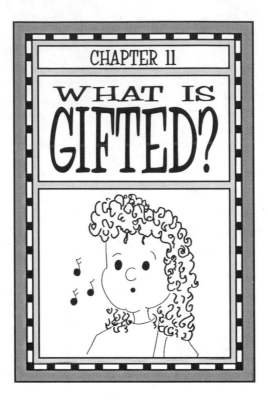

CHAPTER 11

WHAT IS GIFTED?

E ven though Field Day was over and I had been moved back into my classroom, I was still feeling pretty grumpy. Yes, I was relieved not to have to sit at the baby desk in the office anymore. Let's face it though, being grounded at home wasn't much fun. I had decided to be on my best behavior.

As I said before, being in the office made me notice things more. I thought it would be a good idea to write down everything I saw about Rachel. Then, when I was ready to give her a helpful little "push over the edge" onto the road leading to suspension, I would have a whole list of ideas to choose from.

It wasn't hard to get lots of information about Rachel. For instance, Rachel was constantly making noises. I had always thought she was just talking to other kids in class, but I remembered that she didn't really have any friends; she just made noises. She made burping noises, she put her hand under her arm and made pit noises, she whistled, she sang, and she even talked to herself.

After jotting down some notes about noises, I decided to write down some notes about the stuff she brought to school. There was lots to write down in that area, too. Her desk looked like a volcano of garbage that had just erupted. Her books were spread out over the top of her desk. They were covered with crumpled-up notebook paper, pencils, broken crayons, and dirty tissues. Little treasures that she had been collecting flowed over onto the floor around her desk. She also had three plastic spiders, a spray bottle of perfume, and a piece of rubber-coated wire about two feet long. Actually, I wouldn't have minded having the spiders or the wire, but if I wanted them I would have had to ask Rachel, and I certainly wasn't going to get anywhere near her—much less speak to her.

I once did try to borrow something from Rachel. Last year she brought a whole set of colored glue to school. I was working on a poster for art and asked Rachel if I could use her glue. She said, "Sure!" As she handed it to me, she "accidentally" squirted it all over me and my poster.

I decided that my notes wouldn't be complete without a description of Rachel. She was very short—she was a year younger and more immature than the rest of the class. Rachel always told people that she was so smart that her mother said she was "gifted." That's why she started school a year earlier than the rest of the kids in her class. Of course, no way did I believe that story. I figured that if you had a kid like Rachel in your family, you'd do anything to get her out of the house and into school a year early.

After noticing what a shrimp she was, I continued to study her appearance. From head to toe she was truly a mess. Her red hair was a bunch of knotted curls, like she brushed it by swirling it around in a fish tank. Her clothes looked like they had never been washed, *and* they were boys' clothes. Her tennis shoes had no laces. She wore no socks. Her arms and legs were kind of dirty looking.

After school that day I took my notes up to my bedroom to study. I just explained to my mom that I had a lot of stuff to do for school, and she didn't ask me any questions. If all of the real studying I had to do was this much fun, I'd be a straight-A student.

I had three categories to concentrate on: noises, possessions, and appearance. It would be very easy to help Rachel get into trouble in any of these areas. She already disrupted the class, made terrible messes, and always looked like she'd just been in a fight.

"That's it!" I cried aloud. "A fight." The school handbook clearly says that a student can be suspended for fighting. All I have to do is figure out a way to get the other kids mad at her. Then, when a fight starts, everyone will blame Rachel. With the way she looks and after the fire extinguisher incident, the principal will believe that she started the fight.

I got so excited about getting Rachel into trouble, I forgot that I was still in a lot of trouble myself. My mind started racing, trying to form the perfect plan. I realized that if any of my friends or I were involved in a fight with Rachel, I might get blamed. I had to arrange for the girls to get into a fight at school, so Rachel would be suspended. The idea came to me at dinner that night.

Tisha was working on a cooking project for the Girl Scouts, so she had to prepare part of our dinner. She had made the salad. I guessed why Mom had given her the salad to do—how could anyone ruin a salad? Tisha found a way. She made her own salad dressing instead of using the kind that comes in a bottle. As she was pouring the dressing over the salad, she spilled it on Dad's chair. No one had come to the table yet, so Tisha wiped up the spill and didn't tell anyone. She didn't do a great job of cleaning up. When Dad sat down at the table, he slipped right off his chair and landed flat on the floor. I started laughing so hard that I was sent to my room.

When I stopped laughing, I realized that I had the perfect plan. It would take a lot of thinking to work out the details, but I knew I could make it work. I would take some of Tisha's greasy salad dressing to school. When I had the chance, I would spread it on the chairs at the girls' table in the lunchroom. Then I would put the salad dressing bottle in Rachel's mess under her desk. When the girls saw that, they'd surely blame Rachel. A fight was almost guaranteed. I knew I could at least count on Heather to get really mad at Rachel. When Heather started pinching her, Rachel would start slugging; then it would be bye-bye Rachel. I had a new favorite food—*salad*…with lots of dressing!

For Review and Further Thought

- What is Jason's latest plan to get Rachel in trouble?
- Does Rachel deserve to be suspended from school? Tell why or why not.

CHAPTER 12

ITALIAN, RANCH, OR 1,000 ISLAND?

The next morning I was the first one downstairs for breakfast. Besides being hungry, I wanted to get the salad dressing out of the refrigerator and into my backpack before anyone in my family saw me. It was close. Just as I was zipping up my backpack, my mother came into the kitchen. "Why, Jason, you're up nice and early. I'm glad to see that you're being more responsible about getting yourself up and ready for school on time. I know we've had to punish you this year for some of your behavior, but I think you can see that it's helping you become more responsible."

"Sure, Mom," I answered, almost choking on a mouthful of cereal. I was anxious to get to school to put my plan into effect. I grabbed the lunch my mother had just finished packing for me and ran out the door.

"Have a good day, dear," my mother called after me.

I got on my bike and rode straight to Pablo's house. When I got there, Mrs. Rinaldo told me that Pablo had the flu and couldn't go to school. This news made me a little worried that I would have to do everything myself; but I rode off smiling, feeling sure that I could handle it.

Throughout the morning I kept feeling my backpack to make sure that the salad dressing was still there. I was getting pretty nervous by 11:00, when I still hadn't come up with a plan for how to get to the lunchroom alone. But my luck changed. Right in the middle of spelling, the fire alarm went off. I heard it as opportunity ringing loud and clear. Ms. Williams was very surprised by the alarm. She was in such a hurry to line everyone up to get outside, she didn't notice when I sneaked around the corner.

I headed straight for the lunchroom. I looked very carefully to make sure that no one saw me. I tiptoed into the lunchroom, went right to the table assigned to the fifth-grade girls, and started preparing the chairs. I was so happy, I was whistling an old salad dressing commercial to myself. What I didn't know was that Rachel was humming along. I was soon to discover her presence.

Just as I was about to leave, Mr. Cheng walked into the lunchroom. Now, I knew that Mr. Cheng was going to check to make sure the building was empty during the fire drill. I just didn't count on him getting to the lunchroom so fast. "Jason, Rachel, what are you two doing here?"

It was what you could call a double surprise. I didn't know that Rachel had seen me, and I had been concentrating so hard that I hadn't even heard Mr. Cheng come into the room. I couldn't think of anything to say.

Rachel grinned and began to speak, "I saw Jason come in here, and I followed him. He said he was looking for you, that he had to speak with you about Space Camp. I was going to help him look for you, but since you're here, why not sit down and hear what he has to say?" As I looked on in horror, Rachel pulled out one of the girls' chairs for Mr. Cheng to sit on.

"Well, you shouldn't be in here during the fire drill, but I understand your excitement over the contest, so I guess it wouldn't hurt to listen to what you have to say, Jason," Mr. Cheng said.

I wanted to cover my eyes as I saw Mr. Cheng lower himself into the chair. It was all over pretty quickly. Mr. Cheng slid off the chair and onto the floor, just like my dad had done. Only this time, I wasn't laughing. Mr. Cheng looked up from the floor and saw the salad dressing leaking out of my backpack. "Jason, is this your backpack?" Mr. Cheng asked.

"Yes," I answered. I knew at this point there was no use denying it.

"Was Rachel your partner is this ... hmm ... activity?"

"No!" I shouted without thinking. There was no way I was ever going to call Rachel my partner.

"Rachel, go outside with the rest of your class. Jason, in my office, NOW!"

As I walked to the principal's office, I could hear the sound of Rachel Rude Rowdy softly giggling in the background.

For Review and Further Thought

☐ Why do you think Rachel was giggling?
☐ Who do you think has more problems, Jason or Rachel? Tell why.

CHAPTER 13

YOU CALL THIS HELP?

Mr. Cheng's secretary called my parents. She set up a conference for Ms. Williams, Mr. Cheng, and my mom and dad. Like most kids, I would have preferred to get my punishment right away. Maybe that's why Mr. Cheng made me wait until the next day after school. They must teach principals how to make kids suffer, like it's part of their job.

Getting from one day to the next never seemed to take as long as this was taking. I kept trying to imagine what was going to happen to me. I was already grounded. I had missed Field Day. It got to be that every time a grown-up spoke to me, I prepared myself to hear yelling. In a way, yelling would have been a relief. There was no yelling. My parents kept looking at me with worried faces. They didn't say anything to me. Their silence was deafening. It was worse than yelling.

Tisha was the only one who treated me the same as always. "Boy, are you going to get it now. You're going to be grounded for the rest of your life. Way to go, Jay!"

Ordinarily, I would have let her have it. I hated it when she started teasing me in that sing-song voice. I hated it even more when she called me Jay. It was strange, but this time I almost liked being teased by Tisha. It was one of the few things that seemed normal in my life. Things hadn't been the same since I had to sit by myself at the baby desk and miss Field Day.

When I got to school on the day of the conference, even the other kids treated me differently. Pablo was still home with the flu, so I was feeling pretty lonely and sorry for myself. The day seemed to last forever. To show you how bad I was feeling, I even enjoyed the schoolwork. It made the time until the big conference go a little bit faster.

Finally, the bell rang. School was over. Even though I was relieved that the waiting was over, I felt like it was just the beginning of the end. Ms. Williams told me to wait until she got my school records, then we walked to the office together. My parents were seated and waiting for me. I gulped as we were shown into Mr. Cheng's office.

Mr. Cheng began by explaining that everyone was there to try to solve a problem—my unacceptable behavior. I wished the school would spend as much time trying to fix Rachel Rude Rowdy as they did thinking of ways to make my life miserable. They asked me why I acted up and broke so many school rules. I was at a loss. How could I explain myself without getting into even more trouble? I just sat silently in my seat.

I was feeling so nervous, I was afraid I was going to get sick right there in the principal's office. If Mr. Cheng got so mad about a little salad dressing, imagine how upset he'd be if I threw up in his office. I just kept swallowing hard. After a while, Mr. Cheng told me to wait outside so the adults could speak in private. I was relieved to leave that room, but I was also curious.

My curiosity got the best of me. I had to know what they were saying. Fortunately, my in-house suspension finally paid off. The secretary had gone home for the day. I went over to the desk where

I had seen the secretary use the speakers to the classrooms. I found the button marked "Principal's Office." I pushed it down. There was a beep.

Mr. Cheng said, "Yes, what is it?" I held my breath. Then I heard him say to my parents, "That darn speaker system hasn't worked quite right in a long time. Please excuse the interruption."

I could hear everything. Ms. Williams began by explaining how she was studying to be a counselor. She said she had some ideas for helping me with my behavior problems.

"I believe that Jason is a wonderful person, but for some reason he keeps trying to get negative attention," she said. "I've had that problem with another student. Although I can't mention that student's name to you, I can tell you that professional help has made a big difference."

My mother asked, "Could you tell us a little more about this professional help?"

"Yes," Ms. Williams continued, "I can even give the names of a few counseling services to you. They specialize in helping children. Some even offer group sessions. Right now, one is working on forming a group that meets every Tuesday afternoon. The children use art to express themselves. A counselor monitors their progress and guides them to better understanding and better feelings about themselves."

My dad spoke to my mom, "I really don't know what else to do. I think we should give this a try. Jason loves art, and I think he would enjoy a group situation. I'm willing to try anything that will get him back on the right track." My mom agreed.

Mr. Cheng thanked my folks for their cooperation. He explained that I still had to face a consequence for the salad dressing incident. Mr. Cheng told my parents that he was going to get me to come back into the room to explain the consequence to me.

I never moved so fast in all of my life. I turned off that speaker button and dashed over to a chair on the other side of the waiting room. Just as I sat down, Mr. Cheng opened the door and told me to come back into his office.

When I was back with the adults, the principal explained that I would not be allowed to go to recess for the next month. He also told me that he expected me to write him a letter of apology for my actions. After the adults shook hands, my parents and I left to go home.

Sitting in the back seat of the car on the way home, I really wasn't feeling so bad. Missing recess for a month wasn't great, but it was a lot better than I had expected. Writing a letter of apology wasn't going to be easy, but I was truly sorry that Mr. Cheng had slipped off that chair. That wasn't what I had intended to happen at all!

When we got home, my mom paid the sitter who had stayed with Tisha, while I headed upstairs for my room. "Just a minute, son, we'd like to talk to you. Tisha, would you please go upstairs to your room so that we can talk privately with Jason?" My dad's tone of voice was very serious.

Now there's a switch, I thought to myself. Tisha gets sent to her room for doing nothing, and I get to stay downstairs for getting into trouble. I should have realized from my dad's tone of voice that staying downstairs was not going to be a treat, but I was so relieved to have the meeting at school over with, I wasn't paying much attention to the signals I was getting.

Mom began the conversation. "Jason, we have been very worried about you. You've broken rules before, but this year you seem to have gotten out of control. We love you very much, and we want to see you become a happier boy."

I really had to fight hard not to answer with what I was thinking. I wanted to tell them that it would be real easy to make me happier. Taking away my punishments would be an excellent start.

"Your teacher seems to feel that going for professional counseling is necessary, son," Dad explained.

"What do you mean?" I said, pretending that I hadn't overheard the conversation. Actually, as I started to think about the idea, I was kind of mad. "There's nothing wrong with me. I'm not nuts. Rachel's the one who's crazy. She's the one who needs help!" I blurted out loud.

"Jason, what are you talking about? First of all, going for help doesn't mean that there's anything wrong with you. It just means that you will be receiving some help in dealing with life. Lots of people go for counseling. When you have an ear infection, you go to the doctor for help. When you have a cavity, you go to the dentist. This is the same thing. Besides, what in the world does Rachel have to do with this?"

I realized that it was hopeless to try to explain, so I softly answered, "Nothing, may I go to my room now?"

I received permission and walked slowly upstairs. I felt awful! Everything seemed so messed up—and I didn't see how it was ever going to get better. I just threw myself onto my bed and started to cry.

For Review and Further Thought

☐ During the conversation in Mr. Cheng's office about Jason's behavior, Jason's mother says she's worried about Jason and that he seems unhappy. Do you think she's right about Jason? Explain.

☐ How do the adults plan to help Jason? Do you think the plan will work? Why or why not?

CHAPTER 14

RESPONSIBILITY IS AN ART?

My parents wasted no time in scheduling my first appointment. I was to go for my first counseling session right after school on Tuesday. My mother picked me up and drove me there. It was a short drive to the clinic. I wished it had been farther. I wasn't sure what to expect at this clinic, but I didn't hold out any kind of hope for it being very much fun. In fact, I was feeling a little nervous about the whole thing. After all, what would happen if it got around school that I was getting counseling? My mother parked the car and came in with me. She had to fill out a lot of papers that the secretary gave her. When my mother finished the paperwork, a lady wearing a white coat, just like at the doctor's office, came out and introduced herself.

"Hi, you must be Jason. My name is Kelli. I've got some fun activities planned for you. This is the first day that we have our new easels in the art room. Some other children have already started painting. I'd like you to join them. Just find an easel that you want to use and paint anything you wish. We don't have many rules. I'll be around in case you have any questions or feel like talking." Kelli then took me into the art room.

I couldn't believe it. This wasn't going to be so bad after all. I could imagine lots of worse punishments than having to paint pictures! Actually, I enjoy painting. Using a big easel was just about the best thing in kindergarten. I wouldn't admit it to the kids at school, but sometimes I really missed those easels. The art room was very big. There were two kids already painting. I chose one of the available easels and got right to work. I decided to just play with the paints at first, to kind of get the feel of it. First, I made big blue lines going up and down. Then I added red squiggles and huge yellow dots. I was really getting into the design when I felt a paintbrush handle being shoved into my ribs.

"Hey, what is the big idea? That's my easel. I was all set to go. I leave to go to the bathroom, and you steal my easel. Move it, dummy!" With that I received a quick, hard kick in the shins.

I had been so busy with the paints I hadn't seen anyone else around me. Rubbing my shins, I whirled around angrily. I found myself staring straight into a mass of red curls.

"It can't be," I screamed, but it was.

Those curls belonged to none other than Rachel Rude Rowdy. I decided right then and there that I wasn't going to put up with Rachel any longer.

"It's my easel, now," I told her. "And now who do you think is the dummy? You're the one without an easel!"

Rachel started to laugh. "You're the dummy," she said, "you haven't even figured out that a person standing outside of the boys' bathroom can hear everything if the window is open. I got your plans out of the boys' bathroom and put the gum under your desk, before you could get me into trouble. That's just the beginning. Your note to Pablo about your next plan made it almost too easy for me. I really enjoyed pretending to get lost in your house so that I could sneak into your room to get the firecracker. Planting the firecracker in your baton was the part that took genius. And, I did a great job, if I do say so myself. I just kind of 'slipped' into the salad dressing mess. But, I do think I handled it brilliantly...getting Mr. Cheng to sit in that chair."

I was so mad I was shaking. Just as I had my hand formed into a fist ready to punch Rachel, Kelli came running over to us.

"What seems to be the problem here?" she asked.

All of the anger that I felt towards Rachel came pouring out.

"*This* person is responsible for all of my problems. She has ruined my life at school. Now she comes over and tries to ruin my painting."

Kelli was very calm. "Jason, I'm glad you're able to express your anger. It's not good to keep all of your feelings inside of you. However, in order to grow up and be a healthy adult, you need to realize that *you* are the only one responsible for your problems. Learning to be responsible for your own actions is a big part of growing up. Now, what are some ways that you could be responsible for solving the immediate problem of who gets to use this easel?"

I couldn't even think clearly, I was in so much shock from being stabbed with a paintbrush, kicked in the shins, and knocked breathless by the words Rachel had just thrown at me. As it turned out, I didn't have to answer Kelli's question. Rachel was very eager to show off. "Let me explain to Jay how we do things here. After all, this is only his first time."

Kelli gave Rachel permission to continue. "You see, Jay, in life we have to learn to be problem solvers, not problems. As I see it, the problem is that we both want to use the same easel. There are several solutions. We could share. I could choose another easel or another activity. You could choose another easel or another activity. See how easy it is?"

As Rachel finished her imitation of Kelli, I started grinding my teeth. I answered quickly, "I'll go find another easel." It's not that I was trying to be a good sport or anything like that. I just didn't want to take the chance that Rachel and I would end up having to share the same easel.

The rest of my time at the clinic that day wasn't much fun. The other kids started chatting. They seemed to be having a pretty good time. Kelli mingled with all of them, making comments on their paintings and asking questions occasionally. As much as I liked painting, the incident with Rachel had ruined my day. In fact, the way I figured it, Rachel had pretty much ruined my life.

For Review and Further Thought

- ☐ Who is the dummy—Jason, Rachel, neither, or both? Give reasons for your answer.
- ☐ On page 55, Rachel says, "in life we have to learn to be problem solvers, not problems." Is there evidence that she follows her own advice?

CHAPTER 15

IF I WON THE WAR, WHY DOES IT STILL HURT?

The next few weeks were not happy ones for me. I went to school, missed recess, went home, was grounded ... except for Tuesday afternoons when I went for counseling.

Not being allowed to do anything else, I kind of looked forward to those Tuesday afternoons. The painting was fun, even though it didn't start out that way. The second Tuesday I was there, Rachel and I were next to each other, so we had to share brushes. This weird girl named Rosa kept bugging me.

"Jason, can I borrow that brush?" she asked in that same whiny voice my sister uses. "It's just perfect for what I want to do."

Rosa kept taking our brushes. I was starting to get really mad, but when I looked over to yell at Rosa, I saw Rachel painting with the handle of the brush in her nose! I burst out laughing. Of course, Rosa stopped asking to use our brushes.

After that (and after washing off the brush handles), the painting was fun. Rachel and I had established a sort of truce. Don't get me wrong; we weren't friends or anything. We just shared the supplies. Actually, Rachel was pretty good at painting. I'd never tell her, but I did admire her style. I was also starting to like the way she could make me laugh. When I wasn't feeling so angry at her, I had to admit that the crazy things she did were pretty funny.

I was humming a song as I got ready for art therapy on Tuesday afternoon. I had started a special painting the week before, and I was anxious to finish it. When I got to the clinic, Kelli greeted me. She told me that this Tuesday was going to be different. "Instead of painting, you are going to work with a partner. You will be using clay," she explained. "Jason and Rachel, I'd like you two to work over at this station. I've put all the supplies there on the table."

Rachel went right over to the table and started pounding and rolling the clay. I was more cautious. Even though I had accepted that Rachel and I were no longer enemies, I didn't think I was ready to be her friend.

"Come on, Jay, this is great! I'm making some spaghetti," Rachel said to me, "you can make the meatballs."

"No way! That's girl stuff. I'm going to make army men to have a war," I explained. "That's what boys do."

"I hate to be the one to break it to you, Jay Jay, but girls can do anything boys can do. I love playing war. I'll make an army that is going to kill yours. Let's go."

I've never been the type of person to pass up a challenge. I guess Rachel wasn't either. We each began forming our own clay armies. After about half an hour we both had several figures ready for action.

I lined up four army figures and made a bugling sound as a signal to start. Rachel lined up four of her figures. The instant she heard the bugling noise, she moved the largest figure in front of the others.

"This is General Rowd. He's my dad. He's the toughest soldier ever. He and his army are going to crush your army into itty-bitty lumps of clay." Rachel was so serious, she was almost talking in a whisper.

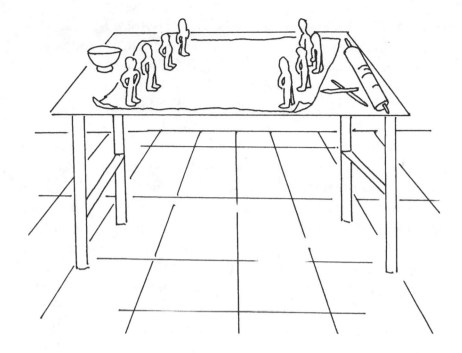

I moved one of my figures to the front. "This is General Parker, my dad," I said. "He and his men will show you what tough is."

Rachel began moving General Rowd to attack General Parker. General Rowd caught General Parker off guard, and knocked him over. Rachel disguised her voice; she began talking as if she were General Rowd.

"Take that, Parker. You think you're so great with your nice new home and your fancy car. I'll show you how important you really are."

I didn't really understand Rachel's conversation, but I did understand playing war. With my right hand I quickly stood General Parker up and began the counterattack. With my other hand, I grabbed another soldier, who began to attack General Rowd from the rear.

General Rowd began to yell commands to his troops. "I need help. Come quickly."

General Parker and his army were clearly winning. General Rowd had become frantic. "I gave a command. You soldiers are worthless. Can't you do anything right?"

General Parker and his other soldiers managed to get on top of General Rowd. In the fight, General Rowd lost his hand. He went screaming back to his soldiers. With his good hand, he slapped the smallest soldier, saying, "You didn't follow orders, Rachel. You are a stupid soldier. You never do what I ask you to do. Rachel, I don't know why I put up with you." Then General Rowd kicked the soldier named Rachel.

I sat, with my mouth open, staring at Rachel. She was crying. "Why did you do that?" I asked.

Rachel rubbed her eyes with the back of her hand. "I was bad. I didn't do what my father told me to do. Then he yells at me. He always yells at me. I try. Sometimes he slaps me and calls me names. I really try to do everything the way he wants me to, but it doesn't make any difference. No matter how hard I try, he just keeps getting mad at me."

"Have you told anyone about this? What does your mother do?" I asked. I was shocked. And I felt sad.

"No, I haven't told anyone; and you'd better not tell anyone either. He's my dad. He can do anything he wants. Besides, you know as well as I do that I'm not exactly what you'd call a good kid. My mom doesn't like it when he acts that way, but when she says anything, it makes things worse. Sometimes he yells at her, really loud. But she told me that he's always real sorry after it happens."

I looked frantically around the room for Kelli, but she had taken another kid into the conference room for a private conversation. When she came out, it was time to clean up and leave.

My mom was waiting to drive me home. In the car she reminded me, "Don't forget that you are still grounded, Jason. When we get home I want you to go straight to your room and start your homework."

I just stared back at my mom with a big smile on my face. Tears came into my eyes. Compared to the battle cries I had just heard, her words sounded like a soothing lullaby.

For Review and Further Thought

☐ What secret did Jason learn about Rachel?

☐ If you learned a secret like that about somebody, how would you feel? What would you do?

CHAPTER 16

IS THERE SUCH A WORD AS "UNGROUNDED"?

uring the next week I did a lot of serious thinking. I was still concentrating on Rachel, but instead of wanting to get rid of her, I was wondering how to help her. I tried to imagine what it would be like to live in a family like hers. I couldn't even picture it.

Ordinarily, I never tell on other people. I've always figured that's what my friends like best about me. But this was different. I had seen TV shows about parents who don't treat their kids right. I knew it was wrong. I also knew I had to tell someone, but I didn't want Rachel to know. After all, she had asked me not to tell anyone.

Just when I was ready to give up on finding a solution, Ms. Williams provided me with a chance. She passed out journals to all of the kids in the class. She told us that our journals were very special. We were expected to write in them every day.

"It doesn't matter what you write. Spelling and handwriting aren't important in your journals. Your journals are private. I just

want you to get in the habit of writing every day. I'll check to see if you are using your journals, but I won't read them unless you want me to. If you'd like me to read your journal, please put it in the tub where you put your finished work. I'll check the tub whenever I get the chance, then I'll return your journal to you as soon as I can. Now, let's begin writing in our journals." Ms. Williams smiled, sat down at her desk, and began writing in her journal.

I bent down very close to the paper. I wanted to be sure that no one, especially Rachel, could see what I was writing.

Dear Ms. Williams,

This is PRIVATE. NO one can know that I'm telling you this. Rachel is in trouble. Her father gets mad at her all of the time. Sometimes he even hits Rachel and calls her names. Rachel thinks he does it because she's bad. I know she isn't perfect, but she deserves to have this problem fixed. I'm not making any of this up. I swear that Rachel told me all of this. Can you please help?

Your student,
Jason

When the journal writing session was over, it was time to go to lunch. Usually I was really quick about getting to the front of the lunch line. This time, instead of rushing to get in line, I told Pablo to go ahead without me. I pretended to have lost my lunch money. While I was searching for my "lost" money, I walked over to the tub and slipped in my journal. I made sure my journal went underneath the other papers that were already there. I didn't want to take any chances on anyone else knowing that I had turned in my journal.

I was the last fifth grader into lunch that day. Usually being last kind of ruined lunch for me. To my surprise, it seemed like the best lunch I had ever eaten.

The afternoon passed very quickly. We were having a science test the next day, so we were reviewing. I'm a whiz at science, even if I do say so myself. Ms. Williams told us to use the last half hour to study silently for our test. As we were studying, Ms. Williams quietly walked around the classroom passing back papers and answering questions. She stopped briefly at my desk. She slipped my journal onto my lap. Pablo was looking at me then, so I put the journal in my backpack to take home.

After school I went right home and up to my room. I took the journal out and read.

> Dear Jason,
>   Thank you for trusting me. I will respect your privacy.
>   Sometimes adults have problems, not just kids. It takes time to find solutions. I will work on finding a solution to the problem you wrote about.
>   You did the right thing by telling me. I am proud of you for caring about your classmate.
>   Your teacher,
>   Ms. Williams

"Jason, do you hear me? What are you doing in there? I've been knocking on your door for the last five minutes."

I looked up as I heard Pablo calling to me from outside my bedroom door. I quickly shoved my journal into my backpack, then opened the door.

"I can't believe you. Today is the first of the month and you're up in your bedroom? Your grounding is history. I already talked to your mom. You're free, man. Let's go!"

Pablo and I were out the door and on our bikes in two minutes. It was hard for me to tell who was smiling the most—me, Pablo, or my mom, who I saw watching us from the kitchen window as we rode by.

For Review and Further Thought

- What did Jason do to try to help Rachel? Did he do the right thing? Give reasons for your answer.
- Why do you think that he wanted to help her?

CHAPTER 17

DIFFERENT?

I felt wonderful. I wasn't grounded anymore. I wasn't getting into trouble at school. My parents had stopped taking me to counseling, because I was doing so well. I had even forgotten about my plans to get Rachel suspended. That's how happy I was. Sure, my sister still bugged me. Now, somehow, even that didn't seem as bad as it used to.

The school was getting ready to have a big science fair. I was really looking forward to it. As I said, I'm a whiz in science. Last year, I won second place for the whole fourth grade. I knew if I worked extra hard, I could win first place this year. Ms. Williams was big on cooperation, so she was going to let us work with partners. With two people working together, I knew I could turn in a super project.

On Monday, Ms. Williams explained the science fair to all of the kids who were new to the school, or didn't remember what it was all about. On Tuesday, the class saw a videotape on how to properly conduct a science experiment. On Wednesday, we did research on different topics that would be acceptable for a science project. On Thursday, Ms. Williams gave a little talk on cooperation and teamwork.

"We can all learn from each other. Different people are good at different things. If you always work or play with the same people, you limit your learning. We go to school to grow. Tomorrow you will be selecting who you would like to work with on your science fair project. In order to help you grow, you need to select someone to be your partner whom you've never worked with before. Also, I'd like you to consider each other's feelings. How would you feel if some-one said 'Oh yuk' when you asked him or her to work with you? Please remember that, boys and girls," Ms. Williams finished.

On Friday morning, as I was locking my bike in the bike rack, Rachel came over to where I was standing.

"Yo, Jay," she said, "how's it going?"

"Not bad," I replied.

Rachel continued, "You know how Ms. Williams said we're supposed to work on our science project with someone different? Well, I figure you're pretty different."

Much to my own surprise, I had to fight off a smile.

Rachel kept right on talking. "Anyway, I thought maybe we could work together."

My mind started working at about 100 miles a minute. What would the guys say if Rachel were my partner? It was one thing to share supplies with her at the counseling center, where no one else could see me. But, here, at school?

"I know you're a genius at science, Jay, and I'm bad at it..."

I didn't even hear the rest of what Rachel was saying. As soon as I heard the word "bad," I knew what I should do in order to feel good. Still, I wasn't too sure if I could actually have Rachel for a partner.

"Rachel, I'll think about working with you on the science project. You are okay at some things. As long as you don't stick a paintbrush up your nose, or anything weird like that!"

Rachel giggled when I teased her. Seeing her in such a good mood, I knew I had the chance to ask her something I'd been thinking about a lot. "I've been meaning to ask you. Remember the army you built and the war we had at the counseling center?"

Rachel looked down at her shoes, "Yeah, I remember."

I took a deep breath and asked, "How is the general treating his army?"

Rachel hesitated, then she smiled slightly. "He's doing better. The general has been going to the counseling center at night. He's learning to treat his soldiers better. My mom and I are okay, too. We're living with Grandma while my mom goes to school. Mom says if she studies really hard, she'll be able to get a job. Sometimes we even do our homework together. Of course, I do have to help her once in a while. My dad visits us when he can. Once he even brought ice cream. I sure am glad he decided to enlist in the counseling center."

As I walked toward the dodgeball area, I grinned and said, "Yeah, so am I."

For Review and Further Thought

- ❏ Some things have changed from the beginning of the story to the end. Has Rachel changed? Has Jason changed? Give reasons for your answers.
- ❏ Have you changed your mind about any of the characters during the story? Why or why not?

MULTIPLE-INTELLIGENCE CHARACTER LESSONS

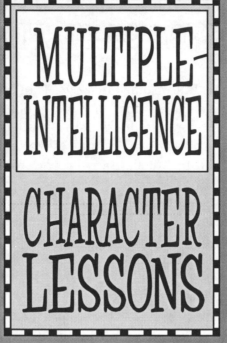

MULTIPLE-INTELLIGENCE LESSON SUGGESTIONS

Everyone is smart, but in different ways. That statement became very real for me as a member of a bilingual team trained to evaluate children for giftedness using multiple intelligences. The Discover program, created by June Maker of the University of Arizona, uses a multiple-intelligence approach for identifying gifted students among minorities.

The very first year we implemented this program, I had a second-grade student, Juan, who I simply could not teach to read. He would sound out a word, *c-a-s-a*. I'd ask him what the word was and he'd say *pollita*. We'd do it again: *c-a-s-a*. "Very good," I'd tell him. "Now say it all together." He'd say *rojo*. I got on the Internet to investigate other teaching methods. I tried everything I could. I'm ashamed to admit that I thought that Juan had limited intelligence.

As we implemented the Discover method, Juan taught me quite a lesson. I discovered that he was a whiz at tangrams (five-part Chinese puzzles). No other student in the room could hold a candle to him. Even the "gifted" student sitting next to Juan asked for his help. Juan had a well-developed logical-mathematical intelligence.

That experience made me a true believer. Everyone is smart. We need to build upon students' strengths in order to shore up their weaknesses. We need to recognize that each child has a gift; each child needs to know that we as teachers value that gift.

Juan gave me quite a teaching gift that day, and it's a gift I intend to pass on to all of my students. For that reason, I have developed multiple-intelligence lessons to accompany each chapter of *Rachel Rude Rowdy*. Use these lessons to help every one of your students learn the important life lesson of tolerance for others' differences. The chart on pages 72–73 identifies and explains the characteristics of the eight known intelligences to help guide your selections for your students.

The lessons on the following pages are intended as suggestions to help you develop *Rachel Rude Rowdy* as a character-building tool in your classroom. Select the activities that fit the needs of your students and complement your teaching style. I've included a few notes about the lessons below.

Timing

The lessons can run anywhere from 15 minutes to an hour, depending on how you adapt them and on your students' responses.

Avoiding Gender Disputes

Be sure to be gender-neutral when assigning groups, positions in debate, and roles in role-plays. Groups could be mixed gender; or boys could represent Rachel's perspective and girls could represent Jason's perspective. Consider various ways to avoid and diffuse "boys-vs.-girls" interactions.

Music

Several lessons suggest the use of music. The use of music and musical instruments is at your discretion, based on what is available and your comfort zone. For instance, music can accompany presentations or serve to highlight specific information or attitudes with, for example, a drum representing conflict and a stringed instrument representing working together.

Naturalist Connections

Look for this icon to make a naturalist connection. You'll find suggestions for adapting a particular lesson to encourage students to use their naturalist intelligence.

There Are Many Ways to Be Smart!

According to professor Howard Gardner, in his book *Frames of Mind* (1983), we all have multiple intelligences. Gardner defines an intelligence as a skill that solves problems or leads to a product valued within a given culture. The following chart identifies the eight known intelligences and lists characteristics of each. Students may be strongest in one intelligence or another, but virtually all intelligences can be strengthened in every learner. Use the chart below to learn about the characteristics of students who may have strengths in a particular intelligence.

Bodily-Kinesthetic

Like baseball star Sammy Sosa and soccer champ Mia Hamm, students strong in this intelligence have a keen body awareness. Physical movement, dancing, making things by hand, and role-playing may come naturally to them. They communicate well through body language and other physical gestures. They can often perform a task after seeing someone else do it just once.

Interpersonal

Like talk-show host Oprah Winfrey and many politicians and social-service professionals, students strong in this intelligence often learn through person-to-person interaction. They generally have lots of friends, love team activities, and are able to show empathy and understanding. Sensitive to feelings and ideas, they are skilled at drawing others out in discussion. These qualities make them good mediators.

Intrapersonal

Like many religious leaders (the Dalai Lama) and artists/writers (Toni Morrison), students strong in this intelligence are self-reflective, self-aware, and highly intuitive. They are frequently bearers of creative wisdom and insight. Inwardly motivated, they may need few external rewards to keep them going. Other people may come to them for advice and counsel.

Logical-Mathematical

Like television personality Bill Nye "the Science Guy" and astronaut Sally Ride, students strong in this intelligence tend to think conceptually and abstractly. Able to spot subtle patterns and relationships, they like to experiment, solve puzzles, and ask cosmic questions. They may enjoy working with numbers.

Musical-Rhythmic

Students with a strong musical-rhythmic intelligence share with pop stars Madonna and Ricky Martin (and composers throughout history) a love of musical patterns. They are very sensitive to sounds in the environment: birdsong, rain on the roof, varying traffic patterns. These students can often reproduce a melody or rhythm after hearing it only once; they may spontaneously sing or compose. Sounds may visibly affect them—look for changes in facial expression and body movement in response to music.

Naturalist

Like primate researcher Jane Goodall and sea explorer Jacques Cousteau, students strong in this intelligence readily notice patterns such as those found in nature. Based on observable characteristics (subtleties in behavior, appearance, texture, sound, smell), they innately sense appropriate categories and are able to group items accordingly. They may like to collect and study items from nature, such as rocks, shells, and leaves.

Verbal-Linguistic

Like civil rights leader Martin Luther King, Jr., and author J. K. Rowling (*Harry Potter* series), students strong in this intelligence are able to connect with and influence an audience using the spoken or written word. They enjoy reading and writing, playing word games, making up stories, debating, and telling jokes. They tend to be precise in expression, love learning new words, and do well on written assignments.

Visual-Spatial

Like architect Maya Lin and painter Jacob Lawrence, students strong in this intelligence tend to think in images. They are often able to discern patterns in shapes, colors, and arrangements of objects. Drawn to visual expression, they may draw, paint, design, or work clay. Tasks that require seeing with the mind's eye (for example, visualizing, pretending, imagining, and forming mental images) may be easy and pleasurable for them.

Adapted from Boggeman, Sally, Tom Hoerr, and Christine Wallach. 1996. *Succeeding with Multiple Intelligences: Teaching through the Personal Intelligences.* St. Louis, Mo.: The New City School, xxciii-xxix.

LESSON 1
KINESTHETIC

Pantomime

Purpose/Objective: Students will identify desirable qualities in a friendship.

Preparation/Materials: You may want to assign partners or groups for this activity.

Steps:

1. Ask students, "Who has a good friend?"

2. Ask why they like their friends. Note these responses on the board.

3. Groups or partners work together to pantomime (silently role-play) how to be a friend. Suggest that students can choose to pantomime any of the responses on the board, or select new ideas such as finding money and returning it, being a good listener, taking turns, sharing, and so on.

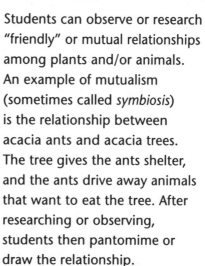

Naturalist Connection

Students can observe or research "friendly" or mutual relationships among plants and/or animals. An example of mutualism (sometimes called *symbiosis*) is the relationship between acacia ants and acacia trees. The tree gives the ants shelter, and the ants drive away animals that want to eat the tree. After researching or observing, students then pantomime or draw the relationship.

Discussion: Ask students to identify the qualities that were shown during the pantomimes.

Summing up: Review the most important qualities a person needs to be a good friend.

Journal: Which of these qualities do you want a friend to possess? Which of these qualities do you possess?

LESSON 2
INTRAPERSONAL

Learning Links

Purpose/Objective: Students will identify different kinds of learning.

Preparation/Materials: You will need strips of construction or colored copy paper approximately 10" x 2".

Steps:

1. Ask your students to tell how they learned to tie their shoes or ride a bike.

2. Pass out strips of paper. Have the students write one thing they have learned at school, but not from their teachers.

3. Glue strips together to form learning links. Hang in the classroom.

Discussion: What do you think Jason meant when he said that he was going to learn a lot that year and that Rachel was going to be his teacher?

Summing up: Looking at the links, sum up all the different ways there are to learn.

Journal: What would you like to learn? How would you like to learn it?

Naturalist Connection

Encourage students to include learning links about the natural world, including animals, insects, birds, fish, rocks, minerals, plants, flowers, stars, and planets.

MI Lessons for Chapter 2

LESSON 1
VISUAL-SPATIAL

Seating Chart

Purpose/Objective: Students will consider and decide what personal qualities go well together when arranging a seating chart.

Preparation/Materials: You may want to prepare and run off a blank seating chart.

Steps:

1. Begin by selecting a student and desribe to the class why that student makes a good neighbor. Ask students to name who they would like to sit next to in class and tell why. You may wish to assign partners and then have students tell in what way their partner would make a good neighbor.

2. Ask why students think you put them in their present seating arrangement.

3. Before beginning, be sure to review ground rules to make sure that no one in the class is left out. Have students create a new seating chart. Have students imagine that Jason, Rachel, and Pablo are also in their class.

Discussion: Did you put together students who are alike or different? Why?

Summing up: Guide students to comment on the importance of diversity.

Journal: If you needed a partner on a school project, would you choose someone like you or different from you? Tell why.

LESSON 2
INTERPERSONAL

Role-Playing

Purpose/Objective: Students will develop problem-solving strategies that incorporate respect for others.

Preparation/Materials: You may want to assign students to small groups for this activity.

Steps:

1. Students form small groups.
2. Each group member should select a character—Jason, Pablo, Rachel, or another student in Jason's class—and take on that role. (Groups can be different sizes; however, be sure one student in each group pretends to be Rachel.)
3. Each group should role-play solving the problem of sitting next to a student like Rachel. (Be sure to emphasize beforehand the importance of treating everyone with respect.) After groups have had sufficient time to practice, they present their role-play to the class.

Discussion: Talk about the various solutions. Which do you think were the best?

Summing up: There are various ways to solve a problem. Review the best solutions and why they were good.

Journal: If you had a problem with someone who was sitting next to you in class, what would you do?

MI Lessons for Chapter 3

LESSON 1
LOGICAL-MATHEMATICAL

If-Then Statements

Purpose/Objective: Students will identify cause-and-effect relationships regarding behavior.

Preparation/Materials: You will need paper and pencils.

Steps:

1. Demonstrate if-then statements by asking students, "If I turn a glass of milk upside down, then _____."(Students fill in the blank.) Do several of these until you are certain all students understand.

2. Review Jason and Pablo's approach to problem solving regarding their annoyance with Rachel.

3. Have students generate their own if-then statements about the characters' actions in the story. Students should then share these with the class.

Discussion: Compare your statements with the way Jason and Pablo are acting.

Summing up: Review what students felt was important in their if-then statements.

Journal: Which statement do you think you might use? Which statement wouldn't you use? Tell why.

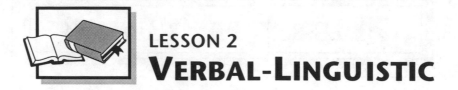

LESSON 2
VERBAL-LINGUISTIC

Crossword Puzzle

Purpose/Objective: Students will identify, define, and use positive problem-solving vocabulary.

Preparation/Materials: Graph paper is ideal for making crossword puzzles.

Steps:

1. Ask students, "Who has ever worked a crossword puzzle?" Explain that the students will have an opportunity to create their own crossword puzzles in this activity.

2. Brainstorm a list of positive problem-solving words (for example: listening, taking turns, cooperation, respect, brainstorming, discussing, sharing, and so on). Demonstrate how to make a crossword puzzle for the class. Younger students may want to list the answers at the bottom of the puzzle. Older students will enjoy the challenge of thinking up the words on their own. All students may need help creating good clues.

3. Students make their own crossword puzzles, trade them with other students, then attempt to solve each other's puzzles.

Discussion: Which words were used the most frequently? (You may want to make a class graph of the results.) Why is it important to use these positive words and demonstrate good behaviors?

Summing up: Effective problem solving requires positive vocabulary and effort.

Journal: Which of the most frequently used words describes how you problem solve? Which one would you like to use more often? Tell why.

MI LESSONS FOR CHAPTER 4

LESSON 1
VISUAL-SPATIAL

Flip Book

Purpose/Objective: Students will sequence events in Jason's gum plan.

Preparation/Materials: Cut many pieces of paper to a uniform size. (Standard size copy paper can be cut into fourths.) Make several sheets available to each student, as well as markers or crayons for drawing. Students will need to staple their books when they are done drawing. Prepare a model of a flip book.

Steps:

1. Ask students what they think of how Jason's gum plan worked. Explain to students that they are going to be examining the steps of the plan more closely to perhaps understand it better.

2. Demonstrate how to make a flip book, showing how repetition and skill in art placement give the impression of movement when

Flip Book

A flip book will work best with from 8 to 16 pages, although students may use more pages. Construction paper can also be used. Students draw each step of their plan on a separate sheet of this paper. The pictures should be drawn in the same spot on each page. The book works best if the first picture is changed slightly or added to in successive pictures.

Have students make a cover for their books. Students should flip through to make sure the pages are in the right order before stapling.

"flipped." Explain to students that they will sequence the events in Jason's gum plan, writing one event per page in their own flip books. This activity will show cause-and-effect relationships.

3. Distribute materials and have students make their books. Students should share their flip books with the class when they are done.

Discussion: Ask students if they can pinpoint what went wrong with Jason's gum plan.

Summing up: What is the result when you make plans to hurt others?

Journal: Tell about when someone hurt your feelings. Do you think he or she planned to hurt you?

LESSON 2
VISUAL-SPATIAL

Posters

Purpose/Objective: Students will identify the importance of rules and showing respect.

Preparation/Materials: You will need poster board, butcher block paper, or construction paper plus colored markers for this activity.

Steps:

1. Ask students: "If Jason and Pablo had followed some behavior rules, would they have ended up in so much trouble?" Ask them to think of rules that would have helped these boys.

2. Have students write their rules as a rough draft. Distribute supplies and have them make posters displaying the rules they would suggest that Jason and Pablo follow. Display posters.

Discussion: Why do you think these rules are important?

Summing up: How can you help people follow these rules?

Journal: How do you feel when you follow the rules? How do you feel when you don't?

Naturalist Connection

The characters in this chapter went to recess. Students can incorporate rules for respecting nature (on the playground or off) into the poster.

LESSON 1
LOGICAL-
MATHEMATICAL

Survey and Graph

Purpose/Objective: Students will investigate which school rules other students feel are important.

Preparation/Materials: Graph paper is helpful, but not essential. You may wish to assign groups or partners.

Steps:

1. Ask if anyone has ever taken part in a survey. Explain that the students are going to conduct a survey of their own.
2. Explain that their survey is about what school rule is the most important. Demonstrate different ways to conduct a survey.
3. Groups or partners work together to plan and survey other students.

Discussion: Students plot their responses on a whole-class graph. (An alternative would be to have each group make its own graph.)

Summing up: Which school rule seems to be the most important to the majority of students?

Journal: Which school rule is the most important to you? Tell why.

Naturalist Connection

Students who created rules for respecting nature in the previous lesson can tally up the most important rules to the class as a whole, then graph the results.

LESSON 2
INTRAPERSONAL

Graphic Organizer

Purpose/Objective: Students will see the relationship between positive behavior and the privilege of independence.

Preparation/Materials: Use a template of a blank graphic organizer (sample sketch below), one copy per student.

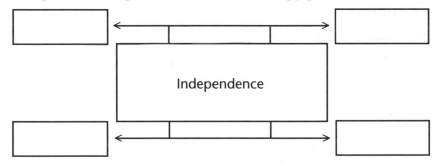

Independence

Steps:

1. Have students discuss what *independence* means. (Refer to the title of chapter 5 as necessary.)

2. Pass out blank copies of the graphic organizers and have students write "independence" in the center box. Instruct students to think of what is connected to independence. (Try to elicit rights and responsibilities.)

3. Students complete the graphic organizers with their personal beliefs about independence.

Discussion: Students share their ideas.

Summing up: Elicit from the students the common factors that they wrote on their organizers. Do the characters in this chapter display any of the common factors?

Journal: Would you like to be more independent? Can you ever be completely independent?

LESSON 1
VERBAL-LINGUISTIC

Poem

Purpose/Objective: Students will contemplate and define the concept of fairness.

Preparation/Materials: Find samples of limericks and/or haikus to share with the class.

Steps:

1. Poll students: "Who thinks that Mr. Cheng's rule that all children can enter a game is fair? Who does not think it is fair?"

2. Explain that students will be writing a poem to show their ideas about being fair. Teach the genre of poetry you will be using (such as limerick or haiku). Writing a class sample poem will help students understand what is expected.

3. Students should write poems about fairness, then share their original poetry with the class.

Discussion: Tell what you liked about your classmates' poetry.

Summing up: Fairness is a concept important to everyone.

Journal: Do you treat others fairly? What is one thing you could do to improve?

LESSON 2
INTERPERSONAL

Developing Group Strategies

Purpose/Objective: Students will consider when it is important to tell an adult something you learned about a classmate and when it is not important.

Preparation/Materials: You may want to assign cooperative groups ahead of time.

Steps:

1. Ask students to stand up if they think Jason's rule about not tattling is good. When they sit down, ask those who think Jason's rule is *not* always good to stand up.
2. Point out that it is not always easy to know when to tell something about someone else and when not to tell.
3. Form cooperative groups. Instruct groups to discuss tattling and to create strategies for knowing the difference between tattling and important telling.
4. Representatives from each group share their strategies with the class.

Discussion: Ask students if they would now answer the initial question differently. Discuss why or why not.

Summing up: Identify the most important and/or common strategies developed.

Journal: How do you feel about tattling? Which strategy presented today will help you the most?

MI LESSONS FOR CHAPTER 7

LESSON 1
BODILY-KINESTHETIC

Partner Challenge

Purpose/Objective: Students will engage in a partner competition to learn the value of teamwork.

Preparation/Materials: You may want to assign partners for this activity.

NOTE: The instructions you will give to students in this lesson are deliberately vague. The natural inclination will be for students to try pulling their partners across the line. However, since both partners pull, there is no movement—showing that working against another person to get your own way does not bring the same quick and good results as finding a way to cooperate.

Steps:

1. Begin by reviewing chapter 7, noting that the characters were engaged in a competition for Field Day. Ask students if they would like to play a game.
2. Have partners stand facing each other, about one foot apart.
3. Partners will draw an imaginary line between them.
4. Explain that the object of the game is to get your partner to cross the line.
5. Begin activity.

Discussion: Ask who won. Share tactics. Did anyone use words to convince his or her partner to cross the line? Did any of the groups feel that both partners "won"? How can working together produce better results? How did you feel when your partner grabbed or pulled you? How do you think your partner felt?

Summing up: What did we learn about making choices and working together?

Journal: Tell about a time when you liked being part of a team effort. What decisions did you make? Why did you like it?

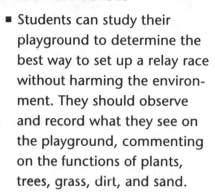

Naturalist Connection

- Students can study their playground to determine the best way to set up a relay race without harming the environment. They should observe and record what they see on the playground, commenting on the functions of plants, trees, grass, dirt, and sand.

- Students can then discuss whether or not Jason's actions might have harmed the environment and how the choices we all make can result in more or less harm.

- Students can generate a list of two possible relay teams composed of insects or animals. They must use classification to make fair teams. (Pitting a team of antelope against a team of turtles would not be fair, for example.)

- As a variation on the partner activity, students could imagine that partners are stuck together in a remote wild setting (on top of a mountain, on an island). They would need to work together to survive.

LESSON 2
MUSICAL-RHYTHMIC

Create Lyrics and Dance Steps

Purpose/Objective: Building character and exploring choices. Students will create a chant to accompany the "Jason Jig." The chant should help Jason focus on building a strong character as well as a strong relay team.

Preparation/Materials: Students will work in cooperative teams. They will need floor space. A variety of musical instruments will enhance the lesson.

NOTE: The use of musical instruments is left to your discretion, based on what is available and your comfort zone. Music can accompany presentations or serve to highlight specific information. See information on music on page 71.

Steps:

1. Review the events leading up to and immediately following the "Jason Jig."
2. Brainstorm what it takes to make a strong relay team.
3. Brainstorm what it takes to build a strong character. Assign teams the job of creating a chant, to be accompanied by movement (for example, dance, cheer, and so on), that would help Jason avoid ending up in the principal's office.
4. Have groups present their chants to the class.

Discussion: Which advice in the various chants is the best? Why? What happens when you follow the advice of the chants? What happens when you don't?

Summing up: Identify common traits listed in the various chants.

Journal: Which of the character traits identified in the chants do you possess? Which trait do you think is most important? Tell why.

MI LESSONS FOR CHAPTER 8

LESSON 1
MUSICAL-RHYTHMIC

Choral Reading

Purpose/Objective: Students will identify the relationship between cause and effect.

Preparation/Materials: You may want to form groups before beginning the lesson. Various musical instruments can be used to accompany presentations or to highlight specific information. (See page 71.) Alternatively, students could use simple percussion instruments such as blocks, or else hum or snap their fingers to accompany their presentations.

Steps:

1. Direct students to hold their pencils above their heads. Next, have students let go of their pencils. Identify which action is the *cause* and which is the *effect*.

2. Brainstorm a list of actions that occurred in chapter 8. Divide the class into small groups, and explain to students that they are going to identify the cause and the effect of the specific actions and/or disagreements in this chapter. They will present these actions by choral reading. When reading the cause, one musical instrument (or sound) will be played in the background. When reading the effect, a different musical instrument (or sound) will be played in the background.

NOTE: Disagreements are likely to arise about which is the cause and which is the effect. This presents a good opportunity for students to practice supporting their statements with evidence or logic. There can be more than one answer!

3. Students prepare and present their choral readings.

Discussion: Ask each group to define the process they used to distinguish between cause and effect.

Summing up: How can you change an effect?

Journal: Have you ever caused something to happen that you would like to change? How would you change it?

LESSON 2
VERBAL-LINGUISTIC

Acrostic

Purpose/Objective: Students will describe honesty.

Preparation/Materials: Blank copy paper and markers (or crayons) are needed.

Steps:

1. Ask students how many know what honesty is. Students should base their responses on their own experiences.
2. Tell students they are going to describe honesty using the format of an acrostic.
3. Demonstrate how to do an acrostic. (Try using *Rachel.* R=rowdy, A=active, C=calamity, H=humorous, E=eager, L=little.)
4. On copy paper, students make their own acrostic for honesty or integrity. Post these in the classroom.

Discussion: Why is honesty important? Is it always important to be honest?

Summing up: Review the most important descriptive words used in students' acrostics.

Journal: How do you feel when someone has not been honest with you? What effects do these feelings have on your behavior?

MI Lessons for Chapter 9

LESSON 1
BODILY-KINESTHETIC

Character Impersonation

Purpose/Objective: Students empathize with characters in the book.

Preparation/Materials: None.

Steps:

1. Ask students how they feel when someone laughs at one of their friends. Explain empathy.
2. Tell students to select one character from the book. They are to impersonate that character and tell how they feel (as that character) about something occurring during this chapter. You may wish to let students practice with a partner.
3. Students should present impersonations to the class.

Discussion: Ask students what they learned about having empathy for the character they impersonated.

Summing up: Guide the students to reflect upon the importance of having empathy for others.

Journal: Give an example of a time when you had empathy for another person.

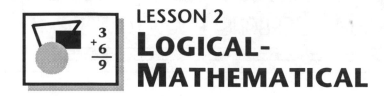

LESSON 2
LOGICAL-MATHEMATICAL

Venn Diagram

Purpose/Objective: Students explore having respect for differences.

Preparation/Materials: Distribute a blank Venn diagram to each student. Students should have pens or pencils.

Steps:

1. Ask students if they have ever felt like Jason, that another student should be "fixed" because his or her behavior is annoying. Initiate a discussion on the pros and cons of trying to change a person versus respecting that individual's differences.

2. Model how to complete a Venn diagram. Distribute Venn diagrams to students and have them label one circle as "respecting difference," and label the other circle as "needs fixing." Have them fill in each circle with words that describe what happens when you respect differences, and what happens when you treat people as if they need fixing. (See example in item 3.)

3. Students should complete and share their diagrams. (If students are stuck, suggest starter words for the "respecting difference" circle: more friends, happier, less fights, and so on. The circle representing "needs fixing" could include words such as boring, judgmental, always late, and so on. The overlapping part would show that the goal of harmony is the same, and perhaps that both ways could lead to more friends.)

Discussion: Which circle presents better choices?

Summing up: Lead students to the observation that differences are often a positive factor in life.

Journal: How are you different? Why is that good?

MI LESSONS FOR CHAPTER 10

LESSON 1
MUSICAL-RHYTHMIC

Skit

Purpose/Objective: Students will identify the characteristics of good citizenship.

Preparation/Materials: You may want to form cooperative groups. Music and musical instruments can be used to accompany presentations or to highlight specific information. (See page 71.) Alternatively, students could use simple percussion instruments such as blocks, or else hum or snap their fingers to accompany their presentations.

Steps:

1. Students explain to their neighbor the opposite of negative.
2. Review the negative behavior demonstrated in chapter 10. Explain to the class that they are going to be doing musical skits demonstrating the opposite of the negative behaviors in this chapter. Positive behavior can also be called *good citizenship.*
3. Cooperative groups prepare and then present their skits.

Discussion: Elicit comments about the pros and cons of positive and negative attention.

Summing up: Reiterate that positive attention that contributes to good citizenship is desired behavior, citing details from the preceding discussion.

Journal: What do you do to receive positive attention? Does it work? How do you feel when you receive positive attention?

LESSON 2
VISUAL-SPATIAL

Collage

Purpose/Objective: Students will identify what they are good at doing in order to enhance their self-esteem.

Preparation/Materials: Suggested materials include old magazines, scissors, glue, and construction paper. You may wish to prepare a model collage about yourself.

Steps:

1. Have students give themselves a hug or pat on the back. Explain that it is healthy to feel good about yourself and like yourself too. Relate this to chapter 10 where Ms. Williams says that poor self-esteem is related to negative behavior.

2. Explain that in this lesson, students will celebrate what they are good at by making a collage.

3. Students make and display their collages.

Discussion: Why do you think it is important to feel good about yourself? When you feel good about yourself, how do you treat others?

Summing up: Make the connection by asking, "When people feel bad about themselves, how do you think they treat others?"

Journal: On a scale of 1 to 10, with 1 being the lowest, rate your self-esteem. Are you satisfied with this rating? Tell why or why not.

Naturalist Connection

- Include photos of natural places and small items from the natural world in the pile of materials available for the collages. Encourage students to consider including naturalist skills, such as caring for animals and identifying/collecting things, in their collages.

- Students can find things in nature that best represent them as a person, and include a drawing or photo of the natural object in their collages.

LESSON 1
VERBAL-LINGUISTIC

Compose E-Mail

Purpose/Objective: Students will evaluate a problem and suggest conflict-resolution strategies.

Preparation/Materials: Computer access is ideal but not essential.

Steps:

1. Review with students Jason's plan to get the girls into a fight. Ask how many think the girls would have fought and how many think the girls would have avoided a fight.

2. Ask students to imagine that they are sending an e-mail message to the girls. Students are to give the girls advice on conflict resolution.

3. Students share their advice with the class.

Discussion: Which advice do you think would actually keep the girls from fighting? Tell why.

Summing up: It is only human to feel angry at times, but there are strategies that can resolve conflicts without fighting.

Journal: Write about a problem you have had that was not resolved in a satisfactory manner. What would you do differently for a better resolution?

LESSON 2
BODILY-KINESTHETIC

Puppet Show

Purpose/Objective: Students will identify and teach other students ways to make friends.

Preparation/Materials: Puppet-making materials can be as simple as body paint and a student's own hand. You could also choose paper plates, construction paper, tongue depressors, socks, or paper bags. Also helpful would be a supply of scraps of material, pipe cleaners, cotton balls, and yarn. Butcher-block or chart paper and a marker are needed for recording the discussion. You may want to arrange students in teams before the lesson begins.

Steps:

1. Pose the question, "Instead of scheming and fighting, how many of you would like to see the characters try to make friends?" Then ask, "Do you think they know how to make friends?" Finally, ask, "How many of you know how to make friends?"

2. Tell students that they are going to create puppet shows that teach children ways to make friends.

3. Students prepare and present their puppet shows. Consider presenting these productions to a younger class.

Discussion: What do you think of the ideas presented? Are they easy or hard to implement?

Summing up: Write on a chart or butcher-block paper as students dictate the main ideas from the puppet shows.

Journal: What is one way of making of friend that you have not tried? Will you try it? What do you think will happen?

LESSON 1
VISUAL-SPATIAL

Mobile

Purpose/Objective: Students will recognize the importance of considering other people when making decisions.

Preparation/Materials: Suggested materials include paper plates or hangers, yarn, construction paper, and markers or crayons.

Steps:

1. Poll students to see how many would make the same decisions as Jason. Then ask how many would make different decisions. Explain that in making decisions a person needs to consider several things. For instance, if the teacher became upset and wanted to keep a student behind after school, what should the teacher consider?

2. Tell students that they are going to make a mobile showing the factors, such as rules, other people's feelings, and consequences, that Jason should consider before making his decision.

3. Students make and hang their mobiles.

Discussion: How would the story change if Jason had considered the factors (social guidelines) on your mobiles?

Summing up: Social guidelines should play an integral part in our decision making.

Journal: Which codes of behavior are most important to you? How do you consider these guidelines when making decisions?

LESSON 2
VERBAL-LINGUISTIC

Speech

Purpose/Objective: Students will evaluate, synthesize, and apply information about kind and respectful behavior to tell how Jason and Rachel could become "we," working together instead of against each other.

Preparation/Materials: Students will need paper and pencils.

Steps:

1. Ask each group of students seated together to collaborate and come up with three important things that have been discussed in the book so far regarding decisions, friendship, and character. Share and discuss.

2. Explain that you wished Jason and Rachel had utilized the information reviewed above. Use questioning techniques to elicit that Jason and Rachel are working against each other. Ask students, "As a reader, do you wish Jason and Rachel would work together?"

3. Tell students they will make a brief speech to the class explaining their plan for changing Jason and Rachel into a "we," working together instead of against each other.

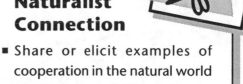

Naturalist Connection

- Share or elicit examples of cooperation in the natural world (wolf packs, elephant herds, ants, bees, bird parents).
- Students can create a recipe of ingredients that go together or "cooperate." Start with examples of recipes having ingredients that *don't* go together, such as sauerkraut and peanut butter.

Discussion: Which ideas or plans do you think are the most likely to succeed? Tell why.

Summing up: It is important to learn how to work together, and generally counterproductive to work against each other.

Journal: Tell about a time you and someone else worked against each other. Tell about a time you and someone else worked together. Which did you prefer and which worked better? Why?

MI LESSONS FOR CHAPTER 13

LESSON 1
BODILY-KINESTHETIC

Signal Game

Purpose/Objective: Students will become more aware of non-verbal signals.

Preparation/Materials: None.

Steps:

1. Stand in front of the class, point at someone, and shake your head. Ask if anyone knows what that means. Explain that what you did was give a nonverbal signal. Ask if it is important to understand nonverbal signals. Ask what happens if you don't understand.

2. Refer to chapter 13 of the novel, where it says that Jason did not pay attention to the signals he was getting from his dad. Emphasize that ignoring nonverbal signals can lead to problems.

3. Explain that the class will play a game to help students get better at reading nonverbal signals. Have one student come to the front of the class and use a signal. The class then guesses what the signal means. Continue the game until you feel students understand the concept of nonverbal signals.

Discussion: What can happen if you don't pay attention to signals? How can reading signals help you?

Summing up: It is important to pay attention to other people and respect what they tell you, even if they tell you in a nonverbal way.

Journal: Think about the nonverbal signals used by someone in your family. Do you notice them? What happens when you do or do not pay attention to these signals?

LESSON 2
MUSICAL-RHYTHMIC

Music to Accompany Art

Purpose/Objective: Students will realize that art and music can express feelings.

Preparation/Materials: Students need drawing supplies to create their own art or a selection of artwork from which to select their own expression of feeling. Students also need access to musical instruments or recorded music. You may want to have art and music samples to model the lesson.

Steps:

1. Ask how many students have ever needed help with something. Connect their experiences to Jason's by reviewing that Jason is going to be getting some help via art therapy.

2. Show different pictures and play various selections of music. Ask students to pair the pictures with the music and describe any feelings the art and music suggest.

3. Give students the opportunity to pair art and music to show how they felt when reading about Jason and Rachel in this chapter. This activity could easily be done in pairs or groups.

Naturalist Connection

- Students can draw pictures of settings (indoor or outdoor) to express particular feelings.
- Students can draw or cut out pictures of pets or other animals that elicit feelings.

Discussion: After each presentation, discuss how the music reinforced the mood created by the art. Have students comment on how they felt during the presentations.

Summing up: Expressing yourself often makes you feel better and leads to better self-understanding. Art and music are good ways to express yourself.

Journal: Which presentation was your favorite? Tell why. How did you feel while looking at the art and listening to the music?

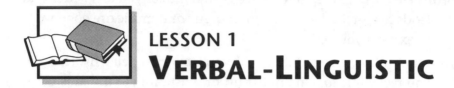

LESSON 1
VERBAL-LINGUISTIC

Debate

Purpose/Objective: Students will see issues from different points of view and increase their empathy for others.

Preparation/Materials: You may want to arrange debate teams before the lesson begins.

Steps:

1. Poll students to see how many think Jason is responsible for the problems in the story, versus how many think Rachel is the one responsible. Record the results of the poll.

2. Explain that students will engage in debates to try to convince others of their point of view. Set rules for debate, such as how much time each side has to talk. Be sure to be gender-neutral in assigning debate positions. (For example, girls can argue on behalf of Jason and boys for Rachel.)

3. Students prepare and present their debates.

Discussion: Poll the students after the debate. Discuss pre- and post-debate results. Why did opinions change or stay the same? Elicit from students that they may understand or empathize with both points of view.

Summing up: It is possible to see things from different points of view.

Journal: Tell about a problem or conflict you have had with another person. Now tell about it from the other person's point of view.

LESSON 2
INTRAPERSONAL

Lists

Purpose/Objective: Students will identify various choices while problem solving.

Preparation/Materials: Students will need paper and pencils. You may want to create a two-column template with one column labeled "problems," and the other labeled "solutions." Each student will need a copy. You may want to assign groups.

Steps:

1. Give small groups a few minutes to collaborate and list the various ways that the problem Jason and Rachel had sharing the easel could have been resolved. Review with the entire class the lists the small groups made.

2. Explain that students will now have the opportunity to individually list problems they themselves have experienced or witnessed. Students will then list different ways each problem could have been solved.

Discussion: Ask for volunteers to share. Ask students to tell you the number of different ways they listed to solve each problem.

Summing up: Problem solving involves choices.

Journal: Select one of the problems you personally have experienced. Tell which of the solutions listed you would choose. Tell why.

MI LESSONS FOR CHAPTER 15

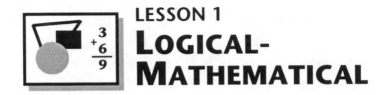

LESSON 1

LOGICAL-MATHEMATICAL

Prediction

Purpose/Objective: Students will utilize what they know about the characters in the story to predict what will happen next.

Preparation/Materials: This lesson describes a buddy method of oral sharing. You may want to assign buddies before the lesson. Alternatively, the lesson can be done by having students write their predictions either by themselves or with a buddy and then share those predictions with the class.

Steps:

1. Explain to students that by now they know the characters in the book very well. Based on what they know, students are going to predict what they think will happen next.

2. Explain that Partner A has two or three minutes to tell Partner B his or her prediction. Then, Partner B talks and Partner A listens. Students will tell the class what their partner predicted.

Discussion: Which prediction was the most popular? Is there a difference between what you want to happen and what you think will happen?

Summing up: Emphasize the importance of using prior knowledge to make predictions.

Journal: How can the skill of prediction help you? Tell about a time when you could use prediction to help you in your life.

LESSON 2
INTERPERSONAL

Analysis and Consensus Building

NOTE: This lesson may be saved until the book has been completed if you prefer.

Purpose/Objective: Students will analyze the story to find a message or moral. They will work together to find a consensus.

Preparation/Materials: Form cooperative groups prior to starting the activity.

Steps:

1. Ask how many students know the story "The Tortoise and the Hare." Discuss the moral or lesson of that story.

2. Explain that there is a lesson or moral in *Rachel Rude Rowdy.* Assign cooperative groups to discuss and ascertain the lesson in the story. Explain that groups need to use their problem-solving skills to come to consensus.

3. Groups meet, and then share their consensus with the whole class.

Discussion: Students comment on the other groups' opinions. The groups share the process they used to reach consensus.

Summing up: If possible, use these processes to come to a class consensus about the lesson in the book.

Journal: How did you feel when your group or class was trying to reach consensus? How do you think students who disagreed with the final decision felt? What personal or class changes would you suggest because of these feelings?

MI LESSONS FOR CHAPTER 16

LESSON 1
LOGICAL-MATHEMATICAL

Timeline

Purpose/Objective: Students will sequence events in the story.

Preparation/Materials: Suggested materials include paper, pencils, markers, crayons, and rulers. Cash-register tape could serve for the baseline to mark the order of events, and index cards or construction paper could be used for recording or illustrating the events. Find or create a sample timeline to show students how to construct a timeline.

Steps:

1. Ask how many think Jason is the same as he was at the beginning of the book. How many think he is different?

2. Comment that so much has happened in the book. In order to understand the change in Jason, explain to the class that they will be looking at all of the events that led up to this change.

3. Show a timeline and explain to students how to make their own. Students then make and display their timelines, showing the events that led to Jason's change.

Discussion: What were the most important factors contributing to Jason's change? Was Jason happier before or after he helped Rachel?

Summing up: People control their own behavior; they make decisions. Decisions that lead to positive behavior make you and others feel better.

Journal: Do you like Jason more before or after he helped Rachel? Tell why. Have you ever helped someone you didn't like? If so, how did you feel? If not, will you try to in the future?

LESSON 2
MUSICAL-RHYTHMIC

Rap or Jingle

Purpose/Objective: Students will celebrate the benefits of having compassion for others.

Preparation/Materials: Musical instruments or recorded music are helpful, but not essential, in this lesson. (See music note on page 71.) Provide pencils and paper.

Steps:

1. Review by soliciting from students how Jason has behaved toward Rachel in the last two chapters. Explain that Jason's new behavior can be described as *compassionate,* a word for caring about others.

2. Ask students if they would like a classmate who shows compassion for others. Do they have a classmate who does that? Who? How has that student demonstrated compassion?

3. Students should write a rap or jingle celebrating compassion. This can be done in pairs or groups. Demonstrate or write a class rap or jingle if students do not understand.

Discussion: After students share their raps and jingles, ask them to talk about compassion.

Summing up: Caring for others is a very important attribute.

Journal: How do you show compassion for others?

MI LESSONS FOR CHAPTER 17

LESSON 1
INTERPERSONAL

Board Game

Purpose/Objective: This lesson can be used as a performance-based assessment.

Preparation/Materials: Manila file folders work well for board games. Light-colored construction paper, oak tag, or poster board would also work. A paper clip can be attached by a paper fastener to an index card to make a spinner, or dice may be used to determine the number of spaces a player moves. Index cards, markers, and crayons would be helpful. You may want to pair or team children before beginning this project.

Steps:

1. Review with students the lessons they have done and what they have learned. Refer to the "summing up" section of each lesson as necessary.

2. Ask, "Who likes to play games?" Tell students that they are going to work in cooperative groups to make a *Rachel Rude Rowdy* board game. The game will be a way to assess what the students have learned. The game should incorporate and demonstrate what the students have learned about character education. Give examples until students understand. For instance, a player could land on a square that says, "Take a Rachel card." The card could say, "You were caught snooping in Jason's room. Go back three spaces for not respecting his privacy."

3. Students make and play their games. This will take a minimum of several days. The game preparation time is the perfect time for you to do part of your ongoing assessment. Document your observations as to how well the students are implementing the lessons they have learned into their daily behavior. Also, note any changes or growth in students you have observed from the beginning to the end of the book.

Discussion: Discuss how the characters in the book have changed from the beginning to the end. Discuss how students have changed over the course of reading the book.

Summing up: Strong character and good citizenship contribute immeasurably to our world and our well-being.

Journal: What did this book make you think about? Did it make you think of something in your life or in another book you have read? Tell about it.

LESSON 2
INTRAPERSONAL

Journal and Ongoing Self-Evaluation

Purpose/Objective: Students will set goals and engage in ongoing self-evaluation. All journal activities are good vehicles for ongoing assessment by the teacher.

Preparation/Materials: Journals. You may wish to provide self-evaluation forms, but this activity could also be accomplished with just a journal.

Steps:

1. Ask who would like to be a faster runner, a better artist, a better singer, and/or a better student. Explain the purpose of setting goals. Tell students that they are going to be writing one or more goals for themselves. Explain that periodically they will be asked to evaluate how they are doing in reaching their goals.

2. Have students write in their journals in response to the following questions: "After reading *Rachel Rude Rowdy*, what character goal or goals can you set for yourself? What will you do to try to reach these goals? How will you know if you are making progress? How will you know if you have achieved each goal?"

3. Periodically, but at least once a week, ask children to evaluate how they are doing. This evaluation can be done on a form you generate or in the students' journals.

Discussion: Are goals important? Why? Are strong character and good citizenship easy or do you have to work at achieving them?

Summing up: Strong character and good citizenship are attributes we need to work on every day.

Journal: What will you do when you feel you have achieved your goals? Will you set new goals? Tell about your decision.

RESOURCES FOR FURTHER INFORMATION ON CHARACTER EDUCATION

Publications

Allman, Barbara. 1999. *Developing Character When It Counts: A Program for Teaching Character in the Classroom.* Grades K–1 and 2–3. Torrance, Calif.: Frank Schaffer.

Boggerman, Sally, Tom Hoerr, and Christine Wallach. 1996. *Succeeding with Multiple Intelligences: Teaching through the Personal Intelligences.* St. Louis, Mo.: The New City School.

Bostrom, Kathleen Long. 1999. *The Value-Able Child: Teaching Values at Home and School.* Glenview, Ill.: Good Year.

Bunnell, Jean. 1997. *You Decide! Making Responsible Choices.* Grand Rapids, Mich.: Instructional Fair TS Denison.

Freeman, Sara. 1997. *Character-Education Teaching Values for Life.* Ages 5–8. Grand Rapids, Mich.: Instructional Fair TS Denison.

Gardner, Howard. 1983. *Frames of Mind: The Theory of Multiple Intelligences.* New York: Basic.

Garnett, Paul D. 1998. *Investigating Morals in Today's Society.* Torrance, Calif.: Good Apple.

Hall, Amanda, Beth Holder, Elizabeth Matthew, Marcia McDowell, Lynette Pyne, Sam Walker, Rachel Welch, and Kathy White. 1998. *Character-Education Ideas and Activities for the Classroom.* Greensboro, N.C.: Carson-Dellosa.

Heidel, John, and Marion Lynon Mersereau. 1999. *Character Education Year 1.* Nashville, Tenn.: Incentive.

Holden, Gerri. 1995. *Students against Violence.* Huntington Beach, Calif.: Teacher Created Materials.

Karsten, Mary. 1995. *Developing Healthy Self-Esteem in Adolescents.* Torrance, Calif.: Good Apple.

Knoblock, Kathleen. 1997. *Character-Education Teaching Values for Life.* Grades K–4. Grand Rapids, Mich.: Instructional Fair TS Denison.

Lipson, Greta Barclay. 1995. *Manners, Please! Poems and Activities That Teach Responsible Behavior.* Grades K–3. 1995. Carthage, Ill.: Teaching and Learning.

Schwartz, Linda. 1997. *Teaching Values—Reaching Kids.* Santa Barbara, Calif.: Learning Works.

Steele, Ann. 1999. *Developing Character When It Counts: A Program for Teaching Character in the Classroom.* Grades 4–5. Torrance, Calif.: Frank Schaffer.

Internet Sites

The Center for the Fourth and Fifth Rs: Respect and Responsibility.
Website by Cortland State University of New York highlights
the center, which serves as a regional, state, and national
resource in character education. Large and informative site;
start your research here. http://www.cortland.edu/www/c4n5rs/

Character Counts! A coalition of national partnerships using Six
Pillars of Character developed by the Josephson Institute of
Ethics. Notable is the section that tells what people are doing
in character education around the United States. In addition,
there is a section in Spanish. www.charactercounts.org/

Character Education Center. Don't miss the Values in Action
section. Each value is thematically linked to a specific body
part to help students develop and remember the concept.
http://www.ethicsusa.com/

Character Education Partnership. Website offers online discussion
of character education. The excellent Resource Center
includes online resource database, information on grants,
and links to articles on the web. http://www.character.org/
reference/index.cgi

*Inside Wake County Public School System: Teachers Fit Character
Education into Their Lessons.* Learn how this North Carolina
school system makes character education a community effort.
http://www.wcpss.net/news/poston/character_education/
character_ed_schools.html

Welcome to Character Education. A website developed by Utah
State Office of Education. Links to great activity and lesson
plan ideas presented by grade level for elementary and
secondary teachers. http://www.usoe.k12.ut.us/curr/char_ed/

Reinforce Student Responsibility and Understanding with These Special Poster Sets

I HAVE A CHOICE
Posters for the Classroom
Illustrated by Stirling Crebbs

Give your students the powerful knowledge of their own ability to choose their responses and actions. This colorful set of eight friendly posters will remind your students to use winning attitudes and behaviors in their lives. Each poster reinforces a specific character trait with an attractive image. Includes—

- Kindness—I choose to be caring
- Perseverance—I choose to believe in myself
- Honesty—I choose to tell the truth
- Optimism—I choose to have a great attitude
- Curiosity—I choose to learn
- Respect—I choose to respect myself and others
- Fairness—I choose to be just
- Self Control— I choose to think before I act

Grades K–5
8 full-color, 11" x 17" posters and annotated bibliography of children's books to reinforce the good choice in each poster
ISBN: 1-56976-135-3
1823-W . . . $27.95

KID SMART
Posters for the Classroom
Created and Illustrated by Donna Kunzler

Put up these bright posters so young students can learn to understand their strengths. Remind students how to use their multiple intelligences with easy-to-understand text and charming graphics. Includes the naturalist intelligence!

Grades PreK–6
9 full-color, 11" x 17" posters
ISBN: 1-56976-136-1
1815-W . . . $27.95

- -

Order Today

Qty.	Item #	Title	Unit Price	Total
	1823-W	I Have a Choice posters	$27.95	
	1815-W	Kid Smart posters	$27.95	

Name _____	Subtotal
Address _____	Sales Tax (AZ residents, 5.6%)
City _____	S & H (10% of Subtotal, min. $5.50)
State _____ Zip _____	Total (U.S. Funds only)
Phone (____) _____	

E-mail _____

CANADA: add 30% for S&H and G.S.T.

Method of payment (check one):
- ☐ Check or Money Order   ☐ Visa
- ☐ MasterCard   ☐ Purchase Order Attached

Credit Card No. _____

Expires _____

Signature _____

Call, write, e-mail or Fax for your FREE catalog!

Zephyr Press

P.O. Box 66006-W
Tucson, AZ 85728-6006
800-232-2187
520-322-5090
Fax 520-323-9402
neways2learn@zephyrpress.com
www.zephyrpress.com
www.i-home-school.com